Terror
ON
Kamikaze Run

Children's Books by
Sigmund Brouwer
FROM BETHANY HOUSE PUBLISHERS

THE ACCIDENTAL DETECTIVES

The Volcano of Doom
The Disappearing Jewel of Madagascar
Legend of the Gilded Saber
Tyrant of the Badlands
Shroud of the Lion
Creature of the Mists
The Mystery Tribe of Camp Blackeagle
Madness at Moonshiner's Bay
Race for the Park Street Treasure
Terror on Kamikaze Run

WATCH OUT FOR JOEL!

Bad Bug Blues
Long Shot
Camp Craziness
Fly Trap
Mystery Pennies
Strunk Soup

www.coolreading.com

Terror on Kamikaze Run

SIGMUND BROUWER

BETHANYHOUSE
MINNEAPOLIS, MINNESOTA

Terror on Kamikaze Run
Copyright © 2004
Sigmund Brouwer

Cover illustration by Chris Ellison
Cover design by Lookout Design Group, Inc.

Published by Bethany House Publishers
11400 Hampshire Avenue South
Bloomington, Minnesota 55438
www.bethanyhouse.com

Bethany House Publishers is a Division of
Baker Book House Company, Grand Rapids, Michigan.

Printed in the United States of America

Library of Congress Cataloging-in-Publication Data Pending
Library of Congress Control Number: 2003023577

ISBN 0-7642-2573-1

SIGMUND BROUWER is the award-winning author of scores of books. He speaks to kids around the continent in an effort to instill good reading and writing habits in the next generation. Sigmund and his wife, Cindy Morgan, divide their time between Tennessee and Alberta, Canada.

For Olivia
and the sunshine you bring
into this world

CHAPTER 1

There is nothing funny—no matter what Lisa Higgins says—about answering the doorbell with a gray wig twisted sideways on your head and a red dress over your blue jeans and T-shirt. Nothing funny at all. Especially when your lipstick is smeared.

"Nice outfit," the man at the door said without meaning it, already wiping his feet on the mat.

"I'm acting a skit for these—"

The man lifted his briefcase and pushed past me.

"—these old folks," I finished to the empty cold wind that blew in from the gray, blustery clouds that hung low and threatened snow.

"Ricky?" As I turned back inside, I could hear Miss Avery's quivery voice call me from the sun-room. "Who is it?"

Good question—for a change. Usually her curiosity drove me nuts. *What are your teachers like? Do any of your friends enjoy playing the piano? Don't you find it cold in here without your sweater?*

I mean, wasn't it enough spending Thursdays here after school without having to make small talk?

That's why I'd allowed my friend Lisa Higgins to convince me to help her with a skit. *"Try to have fun,"* Lisa had said. *"If we're here with these old folks anyway, make the best of it.*" Hard logic to ignore; plus, it's tough to argue with Lisa when she's smiling.

Except, in the middle of the skit, the bell had rung and I'd answered the door in a dress, expecting to find Lisa's aunt returned early with her arms full of groceries. Instead, I'd met the man with a briefcase who hadn't even told me his name.

So I asked him.

"How many old geezers in here?" he replied for an answer. "Place don't seem like much for a retirement center."

I straightened my wig and studied the man. Blue pinstriped suit. Shiny hair plastered over a narrow skull. Long nose. Pinched face. And black eyes that bored into me.

"Geezers?" I repeated.

Funny. How many times have I thought the same word about the people here?

Mr. Barnsworth, who called himself Major and wore a soldier's uniform every day. Gretta Myers, who drooled so much she wore a bib. Mr. Lynch, who hated his false teeth and needed his food chopped soft enough not to hurt his gums. And Miss Avery, with her sad, watery blue eyes and her quivering way of talking and talking and talking. Funny how it now made me bristle inside to hear them called geezers.

"There are four *senior citizens,*" I said, slow and clear.

"And the manager?" the man demanded. "Where's he?"

"She," I corrected. I wondered if he heard the anger in my voice. This was a small center, but I knew Lisa Higgins' aunt did her best to keep everyone happy, especially since they were all in their eighties and needed special attention.

"Yeah. Right. Where's she?" The man tapped the toes of his right foot.

"Buying groceries—" Even as I began, I sensed it was the wrong thing to say. "My friend and I are keeping an eye on things for her."

He smiled. A crocodile smile.

"This won't take long." He began to open his briefcase. "Lead me to them."

"But—"

He was already moving down the hallway. I followed him into the sun-room, where all four residents were enjoying the weak light of a mid-November afternoon. Wheelchairs arranged in a semicircle, blankets across their laps, and Lisa nearby, standing tall beside them with her dark hair bouncing sunlight.

I paused in the doorway to drop my wig and peel out of the stupid dress. The man was already passing out glossy brochures as I caught up to him.

"Fred Norman's the name," he announced. "Making you happy's the game."

Lisa studied one of the brochures. Fred Norman frowned slightly at her but continued his patter.

"You got it, folks," he said in his soothing, oiled voice. "Take a close look at paradise in your hands."

Lisa gave me a searching look. I shrugged in return.

"That's right, folks. Paradise. Warm and sunny all year round."

Miss Avery giggled as she squinted at the brochure. "Oooh. Sounds peachy."

Mr. Barnsworth glared at her. "Peachy? It'd cost a fortune."

Fred Norman saluted Mr. Barnsworth. "You, sir, are a man of obvious intelligence, so I won't try to fool you."

Mr. Barnsworth beamed. I found myself gritting my teeth and hoping Lisa's aunt would return soon. I didn't trust this guy a bit.

"No, sir," Fred Norman said. "A man of your intelligence would know that a retirement home in Florida isn't cheap." He paused dramatically. "Unless some developer has already paid for most of it!"

"Eh?" Mr. Lynch mumbled through his gums.

"Exactly," Fred Norman answered. "Some developer built almost all of the units, then went bankrupt. So the bank is willing to sell condominiums for a song."

He dropped his voice to a stage whisper. "In fact, it's such a good deal, there isn't much time left!"

Mr. Barnsworth brushed imaginary lint from his soldier's uniform. "One must be decisive, I gather?"

Fred Norman smiled another crocodile smile. "One must be *very* decisive."

He reached into his briefcase and pulled out some papers. "In fact, there are barely a dozen units left. And I've been instructed to clear them. Today. For only five hundred dollars, you can get one reserved now!"

Lisa finally looked up from the brochure. "My aunt says salesmen aren't allowed in here."

I nodded agreement. For so long I had thought of these four as problems, old geezers who needed and demanded my time on Thursday afternoons. But these weren't geezers. They were old people, simple and vulnerable in their trust of those who cared for them.

I realized something else. Someday, hopefully a long, long time from now, my own parents would also need to trust others, just like now they were watching and helping me grow up. I was their lamb, and later they would be mine.

And if someday someone tries scamming my parents . . .

Anger hit me at that thought.

"I think you should go now," I told Fred Norman. My boldness didn't surprise me. It was all I could do to stay polite.

"Ask these people if they want me to leave," Fred Norman said smugly.

"Not a chance," Mr. Barnsworth said. "We men of intelligence stick together."

"No," Gretta Myers croaked as she chimed in with her first words of the afternoon. "Mr. Norman is such a handsome young man."

"Five hundred dollars?" Miss Avery added. "It doesn't sound like much."

And Mr. Lynch smacked his lips in agreement.

Fred Norman unleashed a malevolent smile in my direction.

"Enough of an answer, kid?"

He faced the old people. "Five hundred isn't much at all," he confirmed with a smile in Miss Avery's direction. "And the condos cost less than twenty thousand. We make all the arrangements. You have nothing to worry about."

But I worried lots. This guy was charming the bunch of them, and I didn't believe much of what he was saying.

Neither did Lisa. Her lips were pursed in anger. If her aunt didn't return soon . . .

"Ricky," Lisa then said sweetly as her eyes suddenly brightened, "if our seniors want Mr. Norman to stay, perhaps we should show our manners by offering him a snack."

"What!" I almost exploded. *How can she—*

"I'd like my purse, Lisa," Miss Avery said. "This sounds like the opportunity of a lifetime. Imagine, me in Florida."

"My checkbook, too," Mr. Barnsworth said.

Lisa stared me straight in the eyes. "Yes, Ricky, why don't you get some peanuts from Mr. Lynch's room while I get the checkbook and purse."

"But—"

"Peanuts sound fine," Fred Norman said, agreeing to anything just to collect the money.

I shrugged.

It wasn't until I saw the bowl of peanuts on the table beside Mr. Lynch's bed that I understood two things: how glad I was that Lisa had sent me for the peanuts, and because of that gladness, how much I regarded all of these people here as friends. When I returned to the sun-room, everything inside me was hoping Lisa's idea would work.

First I offered the peanuts to Mr. Barnsworth. He looked at me as if I were crazy. Miss Avery refused, politely. As did Gretta Myers. Mr. Lynch waved away his own peanuts too.

I handed the entire bowl to Fred Norman.

He stuffed a handful into his mouth and tried to talk as he munched. "Just . . . *crunch* . . . sign . . . *crunch, crunch* . . . here."

He pulled a sheaf of papers from the briefcase.

Another handful of peanuts. "Folks . . . *crunch* . . . you won't *crunch* . . . regret this."

Miss Avery started to count her money. Mr. Barnsworth started to sign his check.

"Whom do I make this out to?" Mr. Barnsworth asked.

Lisa interrupted. "How are the peanuts, Mr. Norman?"

"Fine," he replied absently. "My thanks to Mr. Lynch."

"No problem," Mr. Lynch said. "I was going to throw them away anyhow." He caught the puzzled look on Fred Norman's face.

"Can't eat them myself," Mr. Lynch explained. "I don't have teeth."

I grinned at Lisa. We couldn't have asked for a better reply.

Fred Norman stopped chewing, looking even more puzzled. "If you don't have teeth, why the peanuts?"

Mr. Lynch waved his hand as if dismissing a silly question. "I love the chocolate."

"What?" Fred Norman slowly swallowed the half-chewed peanuts still in his mouth.

"The chocolate," Mr. Lynch said. "For a snack, Lisa here brings me chocolate-covered peanuts. I suck them until the chocolate is gone and then stick the peanuts in that bowl."

Fred Norman gagged.

"Though why anyone else would eat those peanuts is beyond me," Mr. Lynch finished.

Fred Norman placed a hand over his mouth. What I could see of his face looked as white as death. He gagged again, dropped his briefcase, and bolted down the hallway for the outside door.

I gathered up his papers and snapped the briefcase shut.

"Such a nice young man," Miss Avery said as she folded her money back into her purse. "It's so sad he couldn't stay."

CHAPTER 2

There is something frightening—no matter how innocent you are—about answering the doorbell, even dressed normally in blue jeans and T-shirt, and then looking straight up—way up—into the face of a state trooper who is staring straight down at you.

"Is this the Kidd residence?" the trooper asked. There was no smile below the heavy mustache that formed a drooping line across his broad face.

I could see beyond the trooper to the light dusting of snow that covered the brown grass of our front yard, to the end of the sidewalk I'd just finished shoveling, where his police car was parked on the street. *At least the lights aren't flashing.*

"Um..." I began.

It wasn't that I thought a person should be scared of state troopers. Our town of Jamesville had its own police department, and Sergeant Brotsky often visited our school to tell us about police work. But Sergeant Brotsky never wore his gun, and he smiled a lot. And why would a state trooper from out of town be here an hour before supper?

"Look." His voice was impatient. "I didn't ask a tough question. And I don't have lots of time."

I snapped my eyes away from the holstered gun on his belt.

"Right, sir," I said. "Yes, this is the Kidd residence. But I don't think we've been robbed."

"Is that the paper boy?" my mom called from upstairs. "I'll be there in a second."

I winced at the scowl on the trooper's face as he heard her call him a paper boy.

"Would you like to come in, sir?" I said.

He wiped his shoes on the mat and stepped forward. "I need to speak to Ricky Kidd," he said.

"That's me." I paused, then spoke quickly. "If it's about the water balloons, I can explain."

"Water balloons?" Mom asked as she stepped beside me. "I haven't heard about this yet."

Rats. She could be almost as quiet as my younger brother, Joel, the one who moves like a ghost and follows me everywhere.

The state trooper finally smiled as he removed his hat. Maybe it was the way I was squirming, or maybe it was Mom's own smile at him.

"John Boyd, ma'am," he said. "State Patrol."

"You're not a paper boy," she told him. "My apologies."

"Almost wish I could be," he said. As if he realized how stern he had been, he relaxed slightly, although his voice was troubled. "Less than two hours ago I was measuring skid marks at a three-car pileup on the highway. It wasn't pretty. If only people would wear seat belts."

He shook his head, clearing the memory. "And because I'm in the area, dispatch gives me some grunt work so that an hour later I'm at an old folks' home, trying to take a statement, any statement that made sense. And all of this because the guys in the crime unit are trying to track a real-estate con artist and are too lazy to drive twenty miles to do their own footwork."

"I'll bet your uniform impressed Mr. Barnsworth," I said.

"He never stopped saluting," Trooper Boyd said, now with a sudden grin. "And I know he's old, but there's no way possible he was at Custer's Last Stand, let alone survived."

"It's the history books," I explained. "Mr. Barnsworth reads about all the big battles, and it confuses him a little. You should hear him go on about his cavalry charge in the Civil War."

The trooper started to laugh, then stopped. "I only mentioned an old folks' home. How did you know the one I meant?"

"You asked for me. And that's the only old folks' home I've ever visited. So I made a quick connection."

Mom patted my shoulder. "Officer, this one has a brain that works overtime to imagine connections."

"I see," he said.

There was silence as we waited.

"Oh yes," Trooper Boyd said to Mom. "An extremely pretty girl there insists your son will make a good witness. So I'm wondering if Ricky can join me as I try another round of interviews."

He smiled at my reddening face. I looked for a way to discuss something other than Lisa Higgins. "Is it about Fred Norman and phony real estate?"

Trooper Boyd's eyes widened. "Another quick connection?"

I nodded again.

He stuck out his hand and waited for me to shake it. "I think you'll help just fine."

He placed his hat on his head and nodded at Mom. "He'll be back in a half hour, Mrs. Kidd."

"Good thing, Mr. Boyd. Because two things will happen then. Supper. And my own interview with statements."

"Ma'am?"

"I'm curious to hear what my older son has to say about those water balloons."

CHAPTER  3

"Are you jumpy, sir?"

"Not usually." Trooper Boyd shifted his weight behind the steering wheel to give me his full attention. "Why?"

I thought of the small bootprints I had noticed in the dusting of snow as we had approached the car, bootprints that circled the back end of the police car to Trooper Boyd's side but had not reappeared at the front.

"Because I think we have a passenger."

Trooper Boyd crinkled his brow in puzzlement. Before he could ask the obvious question, I spoke again. But not to Trooper Boyd.

"Joel," I sighed, "it's not polite to hide."

Joel popped into sight from the floor of the backseat and waved a toy pistol. That movement must have been obvious in the rearview mirror, because Trooper Boyd swiveled so quickly that he banged his knee on the steering wheel.

"It's only Joel," I said quickly, because while Trooper Boyd's left hand had grabbed his knee while he groaned, his right hand had instinctively dropped to his holster. "My six-year-old brother and his cowboy pistol."

That should have explained it all, but of course, Trooper Boyd didn't know Joel. I'm twelve, and while Joel is only six, the kid terrifies me. Joel has a knack for knowing the worst time to appear and scare you into a heart attack before silently disappearing again. Walls and locked doors don't seem to stop that kid.

"I'll save us," Joel said as he pointed past us through the windshield at imaginary bad guys. The pistol—a genuine imitation of a Colt six-shooter—was his prized possession. It went with his prized cowboy hat and cowboy boots, because western gunfighters had been Joel's heroes ever since last month when a friend on vacation had visited Tombstone, Arizona, and mailed back to Jamesville a 3-D postcard that showed Wyatt Earp in a shootout.

How many times in the last few weeks had I wished he was still devoted to the teddy bear he used to take everywhere? Too many. I'd already been lassoed from out of nowhere because his imagination had transformed me into an Indian, a cattle rustler, a renegade grizzly bear, or Jesse James. And all his years of practice in following people silently made it next to impossible to know when he'd strike next.

"What's coming at us, Joel?" I asked.

Trooper Boyd was too amazed to interrupt.

"Grizzly," he answered. "Big one."

I watched him draw a bead on his unseen target and begin to squeeze the trigger. Too late I remembered that yesterday was allowance day. *Which means that he's been able to stock up on . . .*

"Joel," I hissed, "don't pull the—"

He didn't listen. The first of his fresh roll of caps exploded as the trigger hammer came down.

Boom! Boom!

In the small space of the car, the normal loud pop of his revolver mushroomed into an earful of sonic pain. Trooper Boyd banged his other knee into the steering wheel.

Boom! Boom!

I grabbed Joel's wrist and pried the pistol from his hand.

"You got him, Joel," I said. The only way to contain him was to go along with his games. "Good cowboys don't waste ammo."

Joel grinned through the trailings of sulfury smoke that hung between Trooper Boyd and me.

"Sorry, sir," I said.

Trooper Boyd took a deep breath, coughed on the fumes of gunpowder, and spoke slowly. "With the kind of day I've been having, this shouldn't be a surprise," he said. "Besides, I've got kids of my own."

He took a good look at Joel. Wide eyes below short brown hair stared back in happy innocence.

"Is it always like this?" Trooper Boyd asked me as he studied Joel.

"Only until he runs out of caps," I said. "That takes about a day."

Trooper Boyd nodded. "Then we'd better let him out here and go to the old folks' home without him. I'd hate to see how much damage he might do to all those unsuspecting old hearts."

CHAPTER 4

Lisa greeted us at the door. "We've been expecting you."

Her polite quietness didn't fool me. Sure, she was easy to look at. Long dark hair, eyes the color of a clear September sky, and a smile that was like the sun breaking out from behind clouds. But I'd also seen the effect of her scowl before—like those same clouds turning into an angry thunderstorm. And I knew how fierce she could be. Once my friend Mike Andrews had teased her about throwing like a girl. She spent two months every day after school pitching a baseball into the playground backstop until she could wing it so hard that the next time Mike caught one from her, it sprained two of his fingers.

So I smiled back at her and hoped I wouldn't make a fool of myself.

"This shouldn't take long," Trooper Boyd told the two of us. "I presume you have everyone gathered, Lisa?"

"Yes, sir. Same room where Fred Norman delivered the sales pitch. And Mr. Lynch is awake this time."

When we entered, it was as if it were still two weeks earlier and Fred Norman had just fled the room with his hand over his mouth. All four of our old friends—I couldn't think of them as geezers anymore—were sitting in their wheelchairs, positioned the same in the room, same blankets over their laps.

Except instead of a con artist, we had the reassuring presence of Trooper Boyd, who now had my full respect for the way he had stayed calm while a grizzly had attacked his car.

Mr. Barnsworth spoke first, saluting Trooper Boyd. "General, so fine to see you again. After last night's shelling, I had feared for your life."

Trooper Boyd spoke his reply in a low voice that was lost as the police radio attached to his belt squawked out some static interference.

"I beg your pardon, General," Mr. Barnsworth said. "My ears are still ringing from the attack."

Trooper Boyd spoke louder. "And I . . . um . . . had feared for your life, too, Major."

Barnsworth grinned. "That fox Robert E. Lee came dreadfully close, but I believe the North shall prevail, even against generals like him."

Trooper Boyd turned to me for sympathy.

"Mr. Barnsworth," I said, "what about Florida?"

"Florida will not fight for the North, young man." Mr. Barnsworth shook his head for Trooper Boyd's benefit. "Nice lad, but dreadfully uninformed."

"Florida," I tried again. "Sales brochures. Fred Norman. Remember?"

"Schales rochures?" Mr. Lynch broke in. He hurriedly popped his teeth into his mouth so he could speak clearly. "Sales brochures. Yes. I know of a way to get a condo for less than twenty thousand. Some developer built most of the units, then went bankrupt. So the bank is willing to sell them for a song. Barely a dozen units left, as I recall."

He paused and looked upward as he searched his memory. "All you need is five hundred dollars down."

Then, because that outburst had taken so much energy, he smiled and let his chin drop down to his chest.

"Why, that's exactly what some young man told us," Gretta Myers added. "If only I could remember his name."

"Fred—" Lisa began.

"—Norman," Miss Avery finished in her shaky voice. "That's why the nice policeman is here again. Remember?"

Gretta Myers shook her head.

Trooper Boyd did not give up, however. "Mr. Lynch, do you have a copy of the sales brochure?"

Mr. Lynch blinked open his eyes. "Yes. I save everything."

Including peanuts after you've removed the chocolate, I thought.

Lisa read Trooper Boyd's mind. "I'll run to his room and look," she said, "if, of course, that's all right with you, Mr. Lynch."

Mr. Lynch might have nodded yes, or it might have been his chin dropping as he tried to sleep again, but Lisa didn't wait to find out. When she returned, she had a handful of papers that she set on a coffee table in front of Trooper Boyd.

He began to shuffle through the stack. Most of it was letters from Mr. Lynch's grandchildren.

"Got it," Trooper Boyd finally announced. He set the brochure aside. "And this, too," he said as he unfolded a long, thin piece of paper which I recognized as the sales contract.

A few seconds later Trooper Boyd let out a low whistle.

"Ricky, describe to me again the sequence of events during Fred Norman's visit."

I retold what I had said on the short drive over. The sales pitch, how Fred Norman had dropped his briefcase after discovering the truth about Mr. Lynch's peanuts, how I'd thrown the papers back inside and left the briefcase outside on the front steps for Fred Norman to retrieve, and how the briefcase was gone when Lisa and I left the home a half hour later.

"Ricky, any chance that you might have missed some of the papers?"

I thought back to the confusion of Fred Norman's exit. Some of the papers *had* drifted onto Mr. Lynch's lap.

"If you're asking if Mr. Lynch could have accidentally picked some up, the answer is yes." I explained why.

Trooper Boyd held up his fingers and crossed them.

"Mr. Lynch?" he said softly.

Lisa gently shook Mr. Lynch's shoulder to wake him.

"Mr. Lynch," Trooper Boyd began again as the old man lifted his head. "Have you ever traveled as Douglas M. Fowler?"

"Not that I can recall, young man. But there was a time in '53 that—"

"Thank you, Mr. Lynch. Maybe this footwork is actually going to pay off," Trooper Boyd said. "Hotel and gas receipts under the name of Douglas M. Fowler."

"Sir?" I asked.

"The guys in the crime division have always been a step behind Fred Norman. The best they could do is get to places like this *after* his visit. And all he'd leave behind was a brochure and the carbon copy of a sales contract that anyone signed. Checks of local motels never showed his name on the registration, and all we've ever had is a description of him. But now—"

Trooper Boyd's grin of triumph erased ten years of age from his tired face. "Now we have the license plate number on his gas receipts and his credit card number from motel stays as Douglas M. Fowler. In the same handwriting as the sales contracts. We've got his real name. It won't be long until the crime division gets him."

Mr. Barnsworth saluted Trooper Boyd. "Fine work, soldier."

Trooper Boyd saluted in return. "Thank you, Major. I must be off—"

"Not yet," Miss Avery said, half in hesitation and half in question. "There is another matter."

"Ma'am?"

I thought of how she loved to talk. Was she going to ask him zillions of questions about police work, just like she grilled me about school? Or was she going to warn him to wear an extra sweater because it was getting so cold now that the first snow had fallen?

"I would appreciate it," she said to Trooper Boyd, "if you could help me with my brother."

Lisa and I shot puzzled looks at each other. Brother? Miss Avery had never mentioned a brother before.

"Yes," Miss Avery said, "I've just received a letter from him and—"

"Where does he live, ma'am?"

"Colorado."

"Mmmm." Trooper Boyd's face showed concern. "Ma'am, it's out of our jurisdiction, but maybe I can offer advice."

She closed her eyes. "I'm so worried."

"Does he talk of a crime?"

She shook her head. "No. In fact, there's nothing unusual in the letter."

"Well, ma'am, is it unusual that he wrote?"

She shook her head again. "He writes twice a month. Has for the last twenty years; he finds it old-fashioned and more comforting than telephones. It's just that—"

She let her voice trail away with worry.

Trooper Boyd's police radio squawked again. The dispatcher rattled off a bunch of numbers. Trooper Boyd grabbed the radio and spoke into it in a low voice. More numbers. Then Trooper Boyd said, "Affirmative."

We all watched him set the radio back in its pouch on his belt.

"I've been called away," he explained. He turned his voice to Miss Avery. "Ma'am. It's impossible for me to do anything about something in Colorado, even if a crime is mentioned. And even the Colorado authorities can't do anything just because you have a strange feeling—"

He stopped as he realized how harsh he might sound. "Ma'am, if you truly believe something is wrong, you might want to consider hiring a private detective."

Miss Avery's voice shook more than usual. "Thank you for your time," she said. "I will look into it."

The radio squawked more numbers and we heard another reply.

Trooper Boyd shrugged his shoulders apologetically. "I've got to run. Ricky, can you find your own way home?"

"Yes, sir."

"Good," he said. "I won't forget your help."

CHAPTER 5

"She may not live past Christmas." Those were the first words Lisa said over the telephone. "She wants us at the hospital right away."

"A lot of people say hello," I told her. "Or even 'Merry Christmas, Ricky Kidd.' A lot of people don't try bad practical jokes."

"It's no joke." Her words were heavy, heavy as the snow that drifted down to cling to the trees outside my bedroom window. Christmas was less than two weeks away, and it definitely looked as if it would be a white one.

"I'm sorry," I said immediately to Lisa. And waited for her to explain.

"It's Miss Avery," she began.

"No," I said, not wanting to believe it. I'd missed the last two Thursday visits at the old folks' home because of school projects. And I'd even begun to miss Miss Avery's endless questions. And now she might...

"Yes," Lisa said. "Meet me there in half an hour."

Miss Avery didn't look sick. Just tired.

The hospital bed around her looked huge compared to her frail body. She was propped against pillows. Wisps of gray hair straggled against the sides of her face.

She smiled as Lisa and I entered.

I tried not to breathe through my nose. Hospital smells aren't fun, and because we weren't here to celebrate, the smells seemed even worse.

"It's okay, Ricky." Miss Avery laughed, and for a moment her wrinkles seemed to disappear. "The air won't kill you."

My face must have showed my reaction at her choice of words. Miss Avery laughed again. "And I didn't ask you both here to mope around and worry about what would be killing me."

I probably flinched a second time.

"Don't worry, Miss Avery," Lisa said. "He's just a guy. They can handle hockey, football, stitches, bruises, and broken bones. It's the serious stuff like feelings that they have trouble with."

Was it that obvious? That I felt uncomfortable being in the same room with someone who might be dying. That I wondered what kind of small talk it would take so that we could all ignore the fact that she knew that we knew that she knew she might be dying.

Miss Avery shook her head and closed her eyes in sympathy at my discomfort. "The doctors tell me my heart has weakened. It may improve. It may not. I'm an old woman. This eventually happens. . . ."

She opened her eyes. "But I'm more worried about my younger brother. And I'd like my mind set at ease. Not only because I want to be sure he is fine. The doctors tell me it may help my heart condition."

I remembered her brief conversation with Trooper Boyd. Jamesville was far too small to have a private detective agency. The state capital, however, probably did. "You'd like us to help you get in contact with a detective agency?"

"No. I—"

"Dumb guess on my part," I said. "The doctors have probably already helped. Or maybe Lisa's aunt."

"No. I *am* capable of dialing a telephone myself."

Now my face turned red.

She laughed again. "It's okay, Ricky. A lot of people assume that becoming old means becoming helpless. Perhaps in some physical things, yes. And I agree that sometimes I blather on and on and ask you questions about school that seem silly to you."

How much redder can a face become?

"But you're such a good sport and so patient that I never minded indulging myself whenever you visited."

Lisa moved to the bed and sat beside her.

I stood where I was, unsure even about where I should put my hands.

"But here I am," Miss Avery said, "making you uncomfortable again, when all I want to do is send you to Colorado."

My head spun. Here was a lady who might be dying and who didn't seem too concerned about it. With a brother in trouble who probably wasn't. And a trip to Colorado thrown into the mix.

Lisa was smiling.

She's in on this, too?

I said as much to her.

"I did know a bit more than you," she admitted from where she sat on the chair. She reached over and patted Miss Avery's hand. "But then, isn't that a woman's job?"

Hah, hah.

"This is crazy," I blurted. "We can't just go to Colorado, let alone go because of . . ."

I stopped myself.

"An old woman's strange feelings?" Miss Avery finished for me.

I nodded.

"You can pull your foot from your mouth anytime," Lisa said to me in sweet tones. "Miss Avery believes she has good reason, and she, of course, knows her brother much better than we do."

I nodded again. *Can having a red face for too long give a guy a bad complexion?*

I finally found my voice. "But why us?" I said. "Especially if there is real trouble. Why not a detective? And who's going to pay? And when will we do it? And our parents would never let us go. And—"

"Hush," Lisa said. "Miss Avery and I have already discussed a lot of this."

I should have suspected a conspiracy.

Lisa counted off her fingers as she listed answers to my questions. "One, we leave on the day after Christmas. Which means we still spend Christmas with our families. That gives us at least a week before we have to return to school. Two, we'll be staying with Miss Avery's brother and his son and family. Which means our parents don't have to worry about us being unsupervised."

"What about the detective part?" I asked. "I mean, in my day-dreams I figure I can get the bad guys, but even I'm smart enough to know they're just daydreams."

"I can answer that," Miss Avery said. "I've given a lot of thought to hiring a detective. But I don't want anyone to know I'm having things checked out."

"He could go undercover," I said.

"But even undercover, he wouldn't be able to visit with my brother and my nephew and his family."

She had a point.

"All I want," she continued, "is someone to be there. Someone to watch and listen and report back to me at the end of a vacation there. Someone to be my eyes and ears."

Report back to her at the end of a vacation there. What if...

"Don't worry," Miss Avery said. "No matter what the doctors report, I won't kick off before you return."

I made a vow to learn how to think without having all my thoughts cross my face.

"And as to the cost," Lisa said, "Miss Avery did make a couple of calls, and she discovered how expensive detective agencies can be."

"Yes," Miss Avery said. "It's far cheaper for me to send you and your friends. Even your brother is going, Ricky. I already spoke to your mother, and she's chipping in to send your brother so that she and your father will have a holiday of their own. They'll keep your sister, Rachel, of course. But your mom did say something about how she's so much easier to look after than two boys always getting into trouble."

Miss Avery smiled.

"Mom was fine with us going?" I asked.

"All I had to do was tell her that Abe, my brother, will be handling your accommodations."

"Accommodations? We're not staying in his house?"

"You didn't know?" Surprise lifted the wrinkles on her face. Then she clucked her tongue. "Of course you didn't. I've never told you. My brother owns a ski resort. You'll be staying in hotel rooms."

I was still thinking that over as she continued.

"As to the friends part," Miss Avery said firmly, "you may be going as my eyes and ears, but I also want you to have fun. And nobody should spend an entire week skiing alone."

It didn't seem like the time to point out that Jamesville did not have a ski hill. Or that none of us had ever strapped on skis before. Or that I'd set aside two days of Christmas vacation to work on a school essay due on January 15.

Miss Avery's cough broke into my thoughts.

"Here, read the letter."

I took the letter that she gave to Lisa to give to me. The type was faded but clear.

```
Dear Helen,
    Things are still fine here in the beauty
of the mountains. As always, I miss shar-
ing them with Myrtle, but often it feels
like she is standing beside me as we marvel
at the beauty of God's infinite power.
    The boys, of course, are fine, too. Peter
and J.P. are growing to look more and more
like their father—a man couldn't ask for
better grandsons, and they ski like they
think they'll live forever.
    As for Robert, he, too, is proud of his
boys and seems to be settling into life as
headman of the resort—
```

I scanned the rest: little details about the resort, some gossip about mutual friends, and at the end, an expression of love for his sister. Nothing that to me would seem to point to trouble worth sending a gang of eyes and ears.

I handed the letter directly back to Miss Avery.

"Lots to worry about there," I said, trying to make a joke. "You sure you don't want to send some marines?"

Miss Avery did smile, then became more serious. "Marines won't do much against a ghost, will they?"

"I beg your pardon?"

"G-H-O-S-T," Lisa said. "Ghost. As in sightings of a ghost and mysterious accidents."

"But the letter doesn't—"

"Yes," Miss Avery sighed. "The letter doesn't say a thing. That's what has me worried."

She handed me a folded piece of paper, obviously torn from a magazine.

"I found this article by accident about two weeks ago," she said. "It's all about trouble at the resort, trouble enough for a three-page piece. Don't you think it strange that Abe would try to keep that news from me?"

CHAPTER 6

"Zebulon," Ralphy Zee said, perched on the side of the hotel bed, with his head bent to read from a book. "Zebulon—"

"Thanks for—two points!—telling us something we didn't already know," Mike Andrews replied. He grabbed a pair of boxer shorts and curled them into a ball. "We've been here at Zebulon for at least an hour already."

Zebulon, as Mike had mentioned without losing concentration on his imaginary basketball game, was the Avery-owned ski resort, a cluster of a dozen buildings scattered on the flat part of a valley bottom, with mountain slopes rising steeply on all sides.

"Yes!" Mike said in mock triumph as his boxer shorts uncurled as they flew through the air to flop in an open drawer. "Another two points. Mike Andrews ties the game and the crowd goes wild!"

I stood by our ground floor window, twirling Joel's toy six-shooter and watching my two best friends. Behind me was the view that had stolen my attention until Ralphy had spoken. Our room was in the building farthest away from the others, and there was nothing to block my view. Mountains, as big as forever. The peaks barely visible in the distance beyond our valley were purple with shadow and haze. The hills of the valley itself were craggy with rocks and snow and stunted evergreens. Even though it was barely four in the afternoon, the sun had nearly set—its last rays bounced off frozen waterfalls across the valley that hung like giant icicles from overhanging ledges.

"Ralphy," Mike said, "your voice sounds like you're dying to unload some encyclopedia stuff on us. Why don't you tell us something useful. Like what *kamikaze* means."

"Where did you get that from?" I asked.

"The brochure on Zebulon. It says that Kamikaze Run is one of the steepest of any ski hills in the entire state. Maybe *kamikaze* is an Indian word for 'try it and die.' "

Mike was at the far side of the room unpacking his suitcase, using the drawer as a basket and his underwear and socks as basketballs. So far he'd scored only six points. The other ten possible points were heaped on the carpet near the drawer.

"Hardly," Ralphy said. "*Kamikaze* is a Japanese term. It means 'reckless, dangerous, or potentially self-destructive.' "

Ralphy was our computer expert, trivia whiz kid, and all around lovable ... well ... geek. As graceful in front of a computer as he was awkward away from one, Ralphy was skinny with brown hair that pointed in all directions. He always seemed dwarfed by the too-large shirts that never managed to stay tucked into his pants, and he had answers for everything. Like this fall when I'd complained about Joel's 3-D Wyatt Earp postcard, Ralphy had told me that concentrated light is so amazing that a split laser beam can be recorded through a couple of lenses, which then refocus the light on film to give an image called a hologram.

Mike snorted as he reached for a pair of socks. "Thanks, Einstein." Mike looked at me. "The brochure says that Kamikaze Run is so steep that often when people fall, they'll slide in their ski suits almost as fast as they were skiing. It recommends that only extremely experienced skiers try that run."

"So that means you'll be on it tomorrow?" I asked.

"Nah. I've never skied before." Mike paused. "I'll wait until the day after."

That answer was no surprise. Mike, too, like Ralphy, always had solutions, but only a brave or foolish person accepted those solutions without thinking. Because Mike had a low tolerance for boredom. If something moved, he tried to stop it, and if it was standing still, he'd do his best to stir it into motion again. His attitude was to fill what was empty, empty what was full, and scratch when it itched. Red hair, freckles, New York Yankees baseball cap, and a grin as wide as a Halloween pumpkin. And, at this moment, not as accurate with his socks as with the last pair of boxers.

"Nuts. Off the rim," Mike groaned as those socks bounced off the edge of the drawer and disappeared beneath the bed. "Time's ticking away. Only three seconds left. He fights for the rebound, steps back and tries the jumper to win the game, and—"

"No," Ralphy interrupted.

"No?" Mike echoed. "No? The great Mike Andrews is about to make basketball history, and you say no?"

"Yes," Ralphy said. "I meant 'no' about what you said about me pointing out the obvious. I didn't mean Zebulon as in here, I meant Zebulon as in 'Zebulon Montgomery Pike.' Where they got the name of the resort and, of course, Pike's Peak. From the army officer who led the first American party into Colorado in 1806."

Ralphy paused as he scanned the page in front of him. "Of course, Colorado wasn't called Colorado back then. You see, the discovery of gold here—"

"Cool," Mike said without meaning it. "Find me a stream. I'll start panning for gold tomorrow."

"Discovery of gold here caused a flood of settlers in 1858," Ralphy continued with patience. "The settlers ignored all Native American claims to the land and proclaimed this area the Territory of Jefferson. But Congress didn't recognize the claim and—"

Mike ran to the bathroom and returned with a white towel. He waved it frantically in Ralphy's direction.

"I surrender," Mike said. "You've managed to bore me into giving up."

"Oh," Ralphy said. He closed his book. A faint look of puzzlement crossed his face. "And I was just getting to the good part. How the

Zebulon ski resort got its name from the abandoned gold mine right below our hotel complex."

"Right, Ralphy," Mike scoffed. "*Below* these buildings?"

"Yup." Ralphy looked upward, a sure sign that he was retrieving data from somewhere in the depths of his brain. "Some of the shafts run a half mile deep. And there is, of course, the legend about the ghost of a miner's daughter who was left behind in the bottom of those shafts. You know, the ghost in Miss Avery's magazine article."

Mike's eyes widened. "Half mile deep? Ghost? I should have paid attention when you guys were discussing it on the plane."

Ralphy faked a yawn. "Of course, if no one around here is interested in the results of my research—"

"Ghost?" Mike repeated.

Ralphy went to his own suitcase on top of the other bed and began to unpack.

"Come on, Ralphy," Mike said. "The towel was just a joke."

Ralphy carried shirts to the closet and hummed while he placed them on hangers.

Mike directed a plea in my direction. "Shoot him, Ricky."

I pointed Joel's six-shooter at Ralphy's back. "Bang, bang," I said without pulling the trigger. The last thing I wanted was to pop the gun caps loudly enough to remind Joel he should come back from wherever he was now and hound me for it to be returned. The pistol, like his teddy bear of old, was my only insurance policy that Joel would stay close enough to be found. I shuddered to think of the alternative, of Joel wandering from building to building in his boots, coat, cowboy hat, and a gun with plenty of blank ammunition, and me with no control over that wandering.

"Guys," I said, "we have more important things to worry about."

"Like what?" Mike said. "Learning to ski? Hah! Give me a day, and I'll blast everyone off the hill."

"No," I said. "Like tonight's supper with Abe Avery and the rest of the family."

"Big worries," Mike said. "I'll mind my manners if you mind yours."

I sighed. "Mike, you know exactly what I meant about supper. We've got to take Miss Avery seriously. After all, it was her money that got us here."

"Okay," he said in a different tone of voice, the one he uses on the rare occasions that he is serious. "But what could we see and hear that would be of any help? I mean, Miss Avery is old and worries about lots, right? And it's not as if a criminal would casually confess anything over peas and potatoes, even if he thinks we're a bunch of dumb kids."

"Correction," Ralphy said. "One dumb kid. With red hair."

Mike grinned at him. "The white towel hurt your feelings, huh?"

Ralphy picked up a pillow.

Mike grabbed one in self-defense.

Ralphy moved ahead.

"Hold it, guys," I said in my best John Wayne imitation as I lifted Joel's pistol. "They didn't call this Colt revolver the peacemaker for nothing."

They didn't even pause as they advanced. Just as Ralphy brought his pillow back, the hotel door banged open, with Joel following it in at a full run, his cowboy hat in one hand as he waved it in my direction.

Joel shut the door behind him and leaned against it, as if he were holding back a legion of monsters. Or, I realized, bandits.

"Fire!" Joel shouted.

I shrugged and pulled the trigger.

Pop. Pop. Pop.

I grinned at Joel. "Who did I shoot now?" I asked. "Bandits?"

He shook his head. "No!" he said. "Fire!"

Pop. Pop. I grinned again.

Joel frowned and shook his head and opened his mouth to shout yet again.

He changed his mind and ran back into the hallway.

"What was that about?" Mike asked.

"Who knows?" I shrugged. "After all, we're talking about Joel."

Mike nodded. Ralphy started to say something.

But I didn't hear a word.

The sudden clanging of a fire alarm deafened all of us, and his words were lost in the overwhelming noise. And I then realized when Joel had shouted "fire," he had not been asking me to pull the trigger of his gun.

CHAPTER  7

"Joel!" I shouted at the top of my voice as he stepped back into the room. "Did you just pull the alarm?"

He raised his hands, showing he couldn't hear me.

I moved closer, past Mike and Ralphy, who now had their pillows wrapped around their heads against the noise. I put my mouth up against Joel's ear and tried again.

"I said, 'Did you just pull the alarm?' "

He nodded, his eyes wider than usual.

Great, I thought. *The desk clerk checks us in, waives all charges, and promises that someone from the Avery family will be by in an hour to pick us up for supper, and before we can even be introduced or thank them, my brother starts a false alarm that will send dozens of hotel guests scrambling outside to stand and shiver in the snow to watch a fire that doesn't exist.*

But now was not the time to instruct Joel on the error of his ways. Not when it took lungfuls of air just to be heard.

It was more important to let someone know this was just a false alarm.

I had two choices. Run to the main building—at least five minutes away after throwing on jacket and boots—or try to yell my message on the telephone above the clanging of the alarm.

Time, I decided, was important, so I moved to the telephone and punched *0* for operator. Except, as hard as I pressed the receiver to my head to hear above the fire alarm, there was no dial tone.

Double great. Joel had probably managed to arrange this, too.

I gestured at Mike and Ralphy to relax and stay put, and then I found my ski jacket. I zipped it quickly, went back to Joel at the door, moved him aside, and pulled open the door to get my boots from the hallway.

A wave of black smoke rolled over me into the room.

Black smoke?

I slammed the door shut. Joel had actually pulled the alarm for good reason.

Now what?

I remembered my sixth grade teacher's favorite expression when we had stupid questions. When in doubt, read the instructions. And in this case, they were posted on the inside of the door right in front of me.

"In case of fire, do not panic."

Triple great. I'd already gotten the first step wrong.

"Move in a calm and orderly fashion toward the nearest exit."

Quadruple great. The map below of the hallway exits didn't do much good if the hall was filled with smoke.

"If the door is warm to the touch, or if there is sign of smoke, do not enter the hallway."

Next plan, then. Panic.

I turned around. Mike and Ralphy were already in their ski pants and jackets. Mike was at the window, trying to open it.

His mouth moved.

I couldn't hear him above the fire alarm.

His mouth moved again.

I shook my head in non-understanding.

He tried it once more.

"It's stuck!" he shouted. This time his voice filled the room, because the alarm had finally stopped.

In its place there was an eerie, low roar. The fire—raging outside. Ralphy grabbed a closed suitcase and ran toward Mike. Mike stepped aside as Ralphy flung the suitcase straight ahead. It crashed through the window and flopped into the snow.

How much time do we have left?

I pressed my palm against the door. It was hot.

"Shoes!" I said.

"Huh?"

I looked at Joel's feet. Still in cowboy boots. He could stand in the snow no problem. But the rest of us were in sock feet, with our boots in the hallway probably already as burned as hamburgers.

"Shoes!" I repeated. Then I thought of the jagged glass in the window frame. "And gloves!"

That low, eerie roar was still growing in strength. And smoke was curling in beneath the door.

Instead of trying to explain, I found my own shoes, then my gloves, and began fitting them on. Mike and Ralphy understood quickly. While they did the same, I was already at the window, clearing pieces of jagged glass with my gloved hands.

I grabbed Joel and lifted him to the window.

He put his arms around my neck and held tightly as I lowered him feet first. When he finally let go, he had only a small drop to the ground.

Ralphy was right behind me. He turned and crawled backward to safety.

Mike was behind him.

But instead of crawling out, Mike handed me a half-filled suitcase.

"Duck, Ralphy!" I shouted and flung the suitcase through. I did the same with the others.

Finally I was ready. I crawled out and fell into the relief of the cold snow. I rolled sideways, and a heartbeat later Mike crashed into the spot I had just vacated.

Already, clusters of people stood around the building. Some were in their ski jackets. Some not. And all stared at the flames rising and dancing through the fast-buckling roof.

Would a normal fire explode throughout the building so quickly? There had been only minutes from the time of the alarm to now, and the destruction was already nearly complete.

Then I remembered a smell that had filled my nose as Joel hugged my neck.

I leaned over and sniffed his jacket, not wanting to believe I could be right.

But my memory had not tricked me.

That same smell was there.

Gasoline.

This fire had been no accident.

CHAPTER 8

"Gasoline?" Hard blue eyes stared at me with the focus of an eagle. "Are you certain?"

This was not the face of someone you wanted to be near when you made a dumb mistake. Not now during supper. Not ever.

I swallowed hard. "Yes, sir." I didn't voice my own questions, because I hadn't yet had a chance to speak to Joel about the afternoon's events. *How had the gasoline reached his coat? How had Joel known about the fire so early?*

Abe Avery set his fork, and the small mound of mashed potatoes it held, back onto his plate. He was a tall man, stooped by the years made more obvious by his silver hair and a lined face that had endured decades of sun and wind. But the skin on those wide cheekbones had no slack or droop, and I'd seen him move around the kitchen with the springy steps of a mountain goat. There were no bulges of fat to fill the red checked lumberjack shirt that he wore. This was no doddering old man. And the fierce glare of eyes shadowed by white eyebrows proved it.

"Joel," he repeated. "That's the little gaffer beside you."

I nodded.

Abe Avery grunted.

I took his next few seconds of silence as disbelief. Lisa, Mike, and Ralphy, also with me at the long supper table, had stopped eating as they measured Abe's reaction, so the silence became heavy.

Behind us, a slight hissing of burning birchwood filled the silence, and light flared from the fireplace, deepening the shadows in the crevices between the thick logs that made up the walls of Abe's house.

Having supper here was like stepping back in time. Only the convenience of electricity in the dimmed lights reminded me that we could step outside to see chairlifts and modern hotel buildings.

Stuffed animal heads—moose and deer—hung from the walls. Snowshoes were pinned in place above the door. A bear rug lay on the floor in front of the fireplace. Old black-and-white photos sat in frames on a heavy walnut desk. Lever-action rifles rested in a gun case.

Abe coughed lightly, taking me away from my study of the room.

"I can get Joel's jacket for you," I said. "I believe you might still be able to smell the gasoline."

His cough continued, and then I understood he had not first coughed to get my attention. His next words confirmed that.

He shook his head when he finished coughing. "Son, I'm not going to insult you by testing what you said. Here in the West, a man's word is a man's word. Not only that, but if my sister thinks highly enough of you to ask me to look after you all, you're the type I can trust."

That trust made me want to blurt out the real reason we were here, but Miss Avery had made us promise to keep that secret because she didn't want Abe worrying that she might be worried.

Abe spoke again. "Gasoline, of course, puts this fire in a whole new light." He thought over his words, then chuckled softly.

"Didn't mean the pun."

That broke the tension. We resumed eating.

Because of the fire, instead of a grand supper with many of the resort guests, there were only the few of us here now. Abe's son and two grandchildren were not able to join us as planned, and even arranging our presence had been difficult. Two hours ago, as the fire had died under the water geysers of fire trucks, all of the hotel guests had been transferred to different complexes. Mike, Ralphy, Joel, and I still shared one room. Lisa, whose room had been down the hall from ours, was now in a different building. Boots had been found for us from the lost and found. We had then been gathered for this supper and escorted by one of the resort employees to Abe's house.

"Didn't notice a ghost anywhere, did you?" Abe asked after another mouthful of ham and potatoes. "A woman in black shrouds?"

He asked the question with such seriousness, we didn't know how to react.

"Dumb question," Abe said in answer to his own question. "None of you arrived until today."

Before I could ask what he meant, Abe set his fork down and leaned forward.

"What did you see, Joel?" Abe asked him. "Right before the fire?"

Joel squirmed.

"He's shy, sir," I explained. "Doesn't like talking much. I was going to ask him the same things later."

"Well," Abe said, "shy or not, he deserves a medal. Spotting the fire so soon gave everyone a chance to clear the building. Who knows how many might have been hurt, or even killed, if he hadn't pulled the alarm."

Joel now beamed.

"Still," Abe continued, "he must have seen something. And I'd sure like to know how the gasoline got on his coat."

"It was on the carpet," Joel said gravely. "In the hallway where I slipped and fell."

I noticed how Mike and Ralphy gaped. They, too, knew how rarely Joel spoke around strangers.

"The carpet." Abe scratched his chin thoughtfully.

Joel nodded. "The fire chased me."

Now it was my turn to gape.

"The fire chased you?" I asked.

"From the towels and alarm clock," Joel replied.

I turned to Abe. "I'm sorry, sir. Back home, he never makes up stories."

Abe closed his eyes.

I waited for him to speak.

Instead, another fit of coughing seized him, and he pulled a hand-kerchief from his pocket to cover his mouth. The coughing fit lasted nearly thirty seconds before he could straighten up again.

He wiped his eyes and managed a weak grin.

"Probably the cold air from all my running around with the fire," he explained. "Blast those accidents."

His face darkened. "And it hasn't been the first, you know."

I felt a slight tingle of anticipation. Maybe there was something to Miss Avery's suspicions about the letter.

Abe Avery nodded, now talking more to himself than to us. "Electrical cables snapped in two, shutting down chairlifts. Kitchen fires. Broken ski equipment. Computer crashes on our reservation system. Three times our central power generator shorted. And I can't tell you how many times our hot water heaters have gone stone cold."

"Sir?"

He snapped back to us, then managed a laugh. "Our skiers haven't been happy when the power shuts down and the chairlift stops and strands them for an hour. Still, some come back because the skiing's so good. And we can muddle through a mess of reservations gone wrong. A lot of skiers still return. And kitchen fires just add a little excitement."

He paused and shook his head sadly. "But lose hot water and it's like we broke their legs. No hot showers, no hot baths after a day of skiing, and our guests threaten mutiny."

He sighed. "I got to tell you, all of this has hurt Zebulon badly. Another season like this and we'd be bankrupt."

He sighed again. "Course, that ain't the worst of it."

We waited.

"It's that miner's daughter. The one dead at the bottom of a mining shaft a hundred years ago."

"I've read about her," Ralphy said quietly.

"Read, nothing!" Abe snorted. "Keep your eyes open, and just like me and a thousand others, you'll see her floating some moonlit night somewhere above the snow."

Abe didn't even smile to show he was kidding. "And after you see her," he said, "expect an accident the next day."

CHAPTER  9

Red, white, and blue, I told myself the next day. *Keep the red, white, and blue in sight.*

It wasn't easy.

The sun was bright, so bright against the pale blue of the mountain sky and the white of the snow that if you didn't wear ski goggles or sunglasses, it was next to impossible to keep your eyes open without squinting.

And I wanted my eyes open wide. That, and the red, white, and blue ski hat pulled down over Joel's ears, was the only way to keep track of him as he dipped and bobbed through the throngs of skiers waiting here at the bottom of the hill to take a chair lift.

To make my task worse, there were so many different colors on so many different ski suits, it seemed like a thousand circuses shaken together and spilled out. And to add to that confusion, this was my first day ever in ski boots and skis, rented at no charge, compliments of Abe Avery. It felt like I was trying to move ahead with long pieces of board strapped to feet wrapped in concrete.

Joel, on the other hand, had adapted more quickly. He pushed his way past taller skiers like a minnow darting among whales.

There were three lineups here. Two led to the chair lifts that carried skiers to the top of the mountain. The third chair lift went only halfway up, to a gentler slope ideal for beginning skiers like us.

Joel, the little turkey, decided to ignore the chair lift we'd been using all morning. He continued on to the next chair lift, a quad, which meant it could carry four skiers up at once.

What to do?

I couldn't let him go alone. If I ever lost sight of him around here, it might take until next Christmas to track him down.

I took a deep breath of frustration and pushed on.

"Joel!" I croaked.

Skiing—or at least trying not to fall as I slowly moved from side to side down the hill—was hard work, and despite the chill of the mountain air, I was hot and tired and thirsty. My voice could barely manage more than that croak.

"Joel!" I tried again.

The red, white, and blue hat didn't even turn to look back. When Joel decided to do something—for whatever reasons entered that mysterious little head—he was stubborn.

I pushed on.

Joel, at least, didn't disrupt things and properly entered the line at the side for single skiers. I managed to reach that line only two behind him.

I panted and leaned forward on my ski poles.

Beside us, the line for skiers in pairs moved forward to the chairs. Our line moved slightly quicker. At the front, the singles joined the pairs to make the foursomes that would ride those giant chairs to the top of the mountains.

As we all moved ahead in rhythm to the thirty-second intervals between the arrival and departure of each quad chair, I stared upward.

The rocky outcrops of the mountain were blue gray, capped with the sugar icing of pure white snow. Clumps of evergreens clung to the mountainside, and higher up the trees became more sparse, so far away that they seemed the size of candles. And, like large winding roadways, the ski runs spilled down the side of the mountains between those trees, with skiers as gliding black dots that traced graceful lines to the bottom.

My eyes shifted back to the red, white, and blue hat in front of me.

Hey, I realized, *Joel isn't waiting!*

The little twerp was getting onto the chair ahead of me, with three complete strangers to his right.

Fine. If he didn't want my company on the way up, see how much sympathy he'd get from me on the way down on these steeper hills.

I moved ahead.

I'd very quickly learned the trick of getting into these chairs. You had to. It was either that or fall off, and then the attendants would have to stop all the chairs all the way up the mountain as they helped you out of the deep snow off the beaten base and back into the chair.

As soon as the wide chair in front had left, you shuffled your skis forward until you reached a line cleared in the snow. You waited in a crouch, and when the chair hit your legs, you sat down and let it lift you.

I'd already done it a dozen times on the other chair lift.

I didn't foresee a problem with this one.

And there wasn't. The great machinery hummed as it turned the cable in a giant sideways wheel above us, a cable that carried hundreds of these huge, wide chairs up the mountain.

Even with three strangers beside me, even with these long, long skis strapped to my feet, I managed to get in the chair as if I'd been doing this since I was a baby. The chair lifted us, and within seconds we were twenty feet above the ground.

Except I'd really messed up.

Because as the chair rose, I heard someone shout my name.

I half turned, looking downward and backward. Mike and Ralphy and Lisa were in the other line waving at me. With a little kid in a red, white, and blue hat standing beside them.

Great.

Why hadn't it occurred to me that there might be more than one red, white, and blue hat somewhere on the hill?

I consoled myself that I really could manage the trip back down these steeper slopes, as long as I went slowly.

I was wrong.

Fifteen minutes later I was at the top of a mountain, staring down between the tips of my skis at a slope that dropped so steeply I might as well have been on the edge of a skyscraper.

CHAPTER 10

I backed up. No sense standing on the edge for a blast of wind to send me out where the birds fly. No sir, I wanted a place of safety to contemplate my upcoming death.

Here at the top, looking east, you could see the jagged slashes of dozens of peaks against the blue sky. I searched for the tallest and told myself it was Pike's Peak, with the city of Colorado Springs on the other side, then started imagining all those thousands and thousands of people in the city, relaxing at home, driving their cars, concentrating on work, none of them scared and alone at the top of a mountain with no way down except for a slippery set of skis with no brakes.

With effort, I shook my head free of those thoughts, then managed to allow myself to look downward. Far, far down, the resort buildings were Lego blocks, dotting the white snow as if scattered by a kid with a temper tantrum. Except one of those blocks was charred black, with the snow stained gray beside it from the ashes carried away by water.

Thinking of the fire beat thinking of who might attend my upcoming funeral, so I rehashed the thoughts that had kept me awake long into last night.

Miss Avery had been right about the letter.

After all, a person would expect Abe to mention stuff as unusual as the accidents and trouble and the ghost. The fact that he hadn't mentioned it said a lot in itself.

On the other hand, what if Abe had decided not to worry his sister, much like she didn't want to worry him by letting him know we were here because she was worried?

Aarrrgh!

That circle of thoughts started to drive me crazy now, just as it had while trying to sleep, so I switched my mind to the fire. A fire that had chased Joel from towels and an alarm clock. I had questioned him about it later, but he had clung to the story.

Gasoline did suggest arson, but even Abe Avery was reluctant to bring this news to the authorities, not with as little to work on as what Joel had supplied us. *Towels and an alarm clock. Hah—*

Then a new thought hit me, one I had not had last night, one that belted me like a blast of wind-driven snow.

What if Abe Avery doesn't want the authorities investigating arson because of the very fact he knows *it was arson?*

I remembered a fire that had shocked everyone in Jamesville a couple of summers earlier. A restaurant fire. The first shock was that it had actually happened—in Jamesville, it was big news if someone crumpled a car bumper.

The restaurant fire had given people something to talk about for weeks. Then, just as it had nearly been forgotten, came the big news. An insurance agency had quietly hired an arson investigation team that finally put the evidence together, evidence that had shown the owner used an oven timer to ignite a pan of cooking oil while the owner was home and asleep.

The reason for the restaurant arson? The owner had been losing money. He decided insurance money would pay him much more than any buyer would for an almost bankrupt business.

Hadn't Abe himself during supper mentioned the resort might go under?

And . . .

I took a deep breath. Because now the normal tone of the letter made sense.

. . . And of course Abe wouldn't mention anything to Miss Avery. He wouldn't want anybody looking too closely at the affairs of the resort, even if that anybody were looking from concern.

And of course Abe wouldn't want what Joel had seen to become public knowledge, because that would also get somebody looking too closely at the affairs of the resort, and that somebody would not be looking from concern but from suspicion.

Again I was chilled by a thought as powerful as wind-driven snow. *If Abe knows that Joel saw something, is Joel now in danger?*

Suddenly I knew I had to get down the hill. I needed to stay as close to Joel as Velcro.

I lurched ahead. But, badly as I wanted down, I couldn't go any farther than having the tips of my skis stick over the edge. How could any sane person launch ahead down this slope? There was at least a mile to the bottom, steeper than any playground slide.

Nobody, but nobody, would—

A dark blue blur whooshed past me as a kid my size whipped over the edge and downward.

I sighed.

"Chicken?" came a voice from behind me.

I started to turn my head, then realized I did not want any sudden movement to threaten my balance, not when I was this close to the edge. So I backed up again, then faced the speaker of that taunting word.

"Chicken?" I squeaked, glad that my sunglasses would not let him read my eyes. "Chicken? Hardly. Just enjoying the view."

I was facing someone almost identical in appearance to the skier who had whizzed past me. My height. Dark blue ski suit. I couldn't see much of his face because his ski goggles covered all of it except for his chin, mouth, and the tip of his nose.

"Good," the kid said. "It's a real pain when skiers ignore the black diamond sign at the bottom of the chair lift. Then we have to call ski patrol to take them down."

"Black—um—diamond." I tried to say it as a statement. Not the question it was.

"Yeah. The symbol for the toughest runs on the hill. And there's no easy way down from here."

He tilted his goggles so that they rested on his forehead. He had a narrow face. Wisps of blond hair were plastered back on the sides of that face. And his mouth became a sneering slash.

"But if I'm explaining black diamond, that means you're one of the geeks who clutter the hills and slow the rest of us down."

Nothing like anger to cloud a person's judgment. Mine.

"Look, pal, I said I was enjoying the view. I can ski with anyone." Not that I planned to start until long after this jerk had left. Another thought occurred to me, and I spoke it. "Besides, you don't own the hill."

"No?" He laughed. "*That's* only a matter of time."

Before I could puzzle out that statement, he moved closer.

"So if you can ski with anyone, pal," he said, "go for it. Hit Kamikaze Run."

Kamikaze Run?

He reached across the small space between us, placed his hand on the small of my back, and pushed.

My skis tipped down as I teeter-tottered forward over the edge. Then I was gone.

A faraway scream reached my ears. I realized it was mine, and that the scream seemed so far away because already the wind pulling it from my throat was the wind caused by going far faster than any human body was designed to go.

CHAPTER 11

All that we had learned in our early morning prep lesson was something the instructor called a snowplow. You turned the tips of your skis toward each other, as if you were pigeon-toed. Then the inside edges of the skis bit into the snow and, depending on where you leaned, either turned you or slowed you down.

So I tried a snowplow.

That was like waving a flag at a herd of stampeding buffalo—nothing slowed down.

Then I thought of falling over. But it was too late. Already I was going fast enough that my ski suit was flapping against the air resistance. I could barely keep my eyes open because the wind was forcing tears into my eyes despite my sunglasses. If I fell now, they'd find parts of me in Utah and other parts of me in Wyoming.

Whoosh!

I screamed past a startled skier who had been making slow, graceful turns ahead of me but who was now a hundred yards behind me.

I realized that I was safe as long as I was on my feet and that all it took to stay on my feet was to keep my skis parallel and shoulder-width apart, squatting slightly so that my knees were flexed enough to absorb shocks.

The only problem was that I had no way to slow down,

and the better I was at keeping my balance, the faster I went.

I rocketed past two more skiers.

A few seconds later the extreme speed made my ski tips flap against the snow.

Then I saw something I didn't want to see.

Bumps. Ahead of me, maybe five seconds away.

Not normal-sized bumps like you'd think the word *bump* should mean. But *mogul* bumps, each one a mini-hill as high as my head, carved larger and larger throughout the season by the turns of skiers at the base of those hills.

I knew when I reached those bumps that I would be dead. Seriously dead.

I was on the groomed speed chute of Kamikaze Run. Little as I knew about skiing, I had seen good skiers from the chair lifts, and I knew moguls were not part of a speed chute but needed to be negotiated with incredible cuts and turns at half speed, much like racing a car on a twisting mountain road instead of a flat prairie highway.

Once I hit the first mogul I would be flung like a rag doll. Even if I landed with my feet first and skis flat, the violence of speed and the fact that I would be landing into the side of another mogul would send me cartwheeling in a circle of arms and legs and skis. With the same momentum as if I had been thrown from a car at freeway speed. And with the same results.

Those moguls started to loom in my vision, and all I could think about was the soft snow Ralphy and I had discovered at the sides of the other ski run, soft snow unpacked by skiers as they avoided the nearby trees, soft snow far deeper than we could probe with upside-down ski poles.

I need to reach that snow—

I need to miss those trees—

I turned my tips. At high speed, I discovered it took little effort for the tips to move sideways. The movement was so easy that I over-balanced, and only a desperate stabbing of my ski pole kept me upright.

Except now a stand of trees filled my vision. I counterturned and felt the tip of a branch slap my arm. I ducked another branch, came through the trees, and discovered I was again moving with the slope of the run. On the side, in soft snow.

Fall, I told myself, *fall now.*

I took the weight off one ski and leaned backward as I tried to sit in the snow powder. I absolutely had to hit the ground butt first. Already in my brief time on skis, I had learned it was the safest way to slide.

Just as I was falling backward, my other ski caught the side of a baby mogul, and in an instant there was no more sound of ski edges whizzing against snow.

I had hit it like a jump and now was in the air.

And screaming.

Because I had been trying to sit, that motion continued, and I felt the flats of my skis against the butt of my ski pants.

I screamed some more.

Then hit ground.

I can't imagine how badly I would have been torn if I had landed tips first to bury my skis into the snow and be flung forward like someone falling over the head of a suddenly stopped horse. But since I was almost sitting on my skis, my downward momentum converted into forward momentum.

This is too much, I told myself as the trees flashed past me in a solid blur of green.

I gave up trying to stay balanced, and I flopped sideways.

After two somersaults, something slammed my ribs, bounced me sideways, and crashed me into a complete stop.

When the world stopped spinning around me, when snow and ski poles stopped beating against me, I opened my eyes.

Blue sky. I'm alive.

Yet something had punched my chest during the fall and had knocked the wind out of me so badly that I could hardly draw a breath.

I concentrated on sucking air, any air.

There was a crunching of ski edges against snow. The kid in the dark blue ski suit blocked my view of the sky.

"Cool run," he said. "But I'm not sure I would have done it quite that way."

I tried to mumble something, but there was no air in my lungs.

He took my silence as agreement and pushed off.

I didn't even have the energy to call him back.

Five minutes later my body still didn't have the energy.

Ten minutes later two members of the ski patrol—large yellow crosses on the back of their ski jackets—arrived and bundled and strapped me into an emergency toboggan that they promised me they could move slowly down the hill with plenty of side-to-side skiing to keep the speed down.

It seemed dangerous, but I relaxed almost immediately. The toboggan was held by ropes attached to the back of it. They stayed uphill, let the toboggan drag them downward, and both of them had a firm grip on the rope.

It should have been very safe.

Except twelve minutes later the rope broke where it was attached to the toboggan.

Ten seconds after that the toboggan was a ski rocket, with me a helpless passenger.

A heartbeat later the large crash that filled my world slammed me into the relief of darkness.

CHAPTER 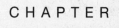 12

I woke to ammonia and blurry flashing lights.

"Urruughh," I said. What I had wanted to come out of my mouth was, "That stuff is awful and where am I?"

More ammonia.

Then my eyes began to focus. The flashing lights belonged to an ambulance. A man beside me was waving something under my nose. And my head hurt.

"Relax," the man said. He pulled the smelling salts capsule away from me.

Like I had a choice? I felt like mushed Jell-O.

Another man, wearing white pants and a paramedic's jacket like the first, appeared in my vision.

"That's right, son," the second man said. "Relax. We'll have you in a hospital soon."

"Hospital?" I croaked. My head hurt, but other than that I was so weak I couldn't feel any major damage. I tried checking my arms and legs to see if they hurt when I moved them.

Nothing happened!

"I'm paralyzed," I moaned.

The first man laughed. "Not quite, son. You're strapped to a stretcher."

I lifted my head to look down at my body. The pain nearly made me pass out, but it was worth the effort to discover the man was not lying.

"Oh," I said. A person is not at his conversational best at these sorts of moments.

They unstrapped me and set me onto a bed with wheels and pushed me into the back of the ambulance. The first man left and climbed into the driver's seat. The second man stayed with me.

"We think you might have a concussion," he said as the ambulance moved ahead. "But probably nothing else major."

"Probably?" Probably is not a comforting word when it involves possible damage to your body.

He chuckled at me. He was middle-aged and balding, with a wide, round face. "We've seen a lot worse, son. Bones sticking out of ski pants, arms twisted backward, legs—"

"Um, sir? I think I get the picture." Even speaking in sentences hurt, but at least it stopped his descriptions.

The ambulance hit a few bumps, then smoothed. We were off the parking lot now and onto the paved road that led away from Zebulon.

The man began to hum.

"Will someone tell my friends?" I asked a few minutes later. It had taken that long to get the energy to speak again.

"You'll probably be back before they finish their ski day. And the ski patrol people are leaving messages that will reach them."

He hummed more. The noise became a buzz in my head, so I interrupted again.

"Which hospital?"

"The closest one. About forty minutes away."

"Oh."

" 'Course," he said, "if this were a real emergency, we could be there in twenty-five minutes."

"Oh."

"But like I said, you're not a real emergency. No sense risking an accident. Some emergencies though—" He looked upward, searching his memory. "There was this two-car pileup once, just north of here. You should have seen those bodies and—"

"Do you have water?" Anything, just to get him away from his gruesome scrapbook of memories.

"Sure."

He found a plastic bottle and brought the nozzle to my mouth. I drank deeply. Gulping hurt, too.

"Thank you."

"No problem."

He set the bottle back and began to hum again.

We turned to enter the main highway. The ambulance rocked and swayed as it picked up speed.

"Jed, our driver, could make this trip blindfolded," the man commented.

"Oh?" I waited for him to begin more horror stories.

"Yeah. I'll bet we've been out to Zebulon four times a week since the beginning of the season."

"That's not normal?"

"Nah. There's a couple other resorts that you might get called to once a week, if that."

"Oh."

The man shook his head. "It's to the point that I'd almost believe the ghost stories myself."

I found the strength to get very interested. "Gold miner's daughter?"

"You've seen her?" His eyes grew shiny.

I started to shake my head no, felt how much that movement would hurt, and changed my mind. "I haven't seen the ghost," I said, choosing my words slowly so that the movement of my jaw was bearable. "But I've heard about her."

"Ghosts and accidents," he said firmly. "Lots of people are starting to stay away from Zebulon. That's too bad. Old man Avery has been here forever. He put a lot of work into building up the resort."

I was prepared to listen now. Anything I could discover about Abe Avery would help.

"Yeah," the man said with enthusiasm. "I heard stories about how difficult it was when he started building his first chair lift. Workers falling from cliffs—"

I faked a smile. "A paramedic's dream come true?"

He smiled back, but his wasn't fake. "Yeah. What I heard was—"

I groaned and closed my eyes. Maybe if I pretended to be asleep, he would keep all that enthusiasm for his work to himself.

"I'll probably be able to get a part in horror movies," I told Dr. James without joy.

He looked up from my ribs. I was glad that it was warm in the examining room and that there were few nurses around. Bare-chested in public is not the most fun way to spend a half-day of your Christmas vacation.

"No stitches," Dr. James said. A slight smile crossed his face. "So that rules out Frankenstein."

"But not The Mummy," I told him, wincing as he pulled the first wrap of a wide cloth bandage tighter around my chest. "I could be The Son of the Mummy."

Dr. James smiled wider. By the laugh lines on his face, I guessed he did that a lot. He was an older man. Short-cropped gray hair. Kindly blue eyes. And—fortunately, because he had probed and poked me about everywhere possible—warm hands.

He ran his fingers down my ribs. "As I said, you'll be bruised some. And the X rays show no broken ribs. I'm guessing it's cartilage damage. That often happens when the wind is knocked out of you. This bandage is just meant to limit any more shifting of the ribs."

"No problem," I said. "With or without the wrap, it was tough to breathe anyway."

This time his smile became laughter. "It's a miracle you're alive with only a slight concussion. I'm glad you're taking it this well."

"Miracle?" I said. "Miracle? *Double* miracle."

I explained miracle number one, surviving the first fall. Then I told him about miracle number two, surviving the runaway emergency sled.

"What did you hit?" he asked.

I shrugged.

He caught the pain on my face and smiled again. "You'll learn not to do that."

"I believe you," I said. I still felt as if I'd been kicked back and forth by giant horses. "And I don't know what I hit. My eyes were closed."

"Mmmm."

Dr. James lapsed back into silence as he adjusted the bandages wrapped around my head.

He kept his fingers moving as he spoke again. "I've never heard of a ski accident like a runaway sled. The ski patrol people always make sure their equipment is in top shape."

I would have nodded, except his fingers were still on my head.

"In fact, there seems to have been quite a batch of strange accidents out there."

Exactly what the ambulance guy had been saying.

For a moment I wondered if my accident had been an accident. What if . . .

I didn't even finish that thought, because a new one replaced it so quickly.

No, I told myself, *dumb idea.*

Why not, I asked myself.

I considered it, silently argued with myself, then realized it wouldn't hurt to try.

"About my broken leg," I began.

"Broken leg? But there's nothing wrong with your—"

"Have you ever had a friend try to throw a worm in your mouth?" I asked, referring to something Mike Andrews had done to me once. "Or have you ever shown up at a birthday party dressed as a clown because that same friend told you it was a costume party . . . and it wasn't?"

Dr. James didn't understand what direction I was headed with my questions, but he was smiling.

"Have you ever had that friend trick you into eating Tabasco sauce? Or fool you into thinking a ghost was outside your window?

Put catnip in your pillow so that you'd wake up with a cat on your face?"

Dr. James grinned from ear to ear as he shook his head in mock disbelief.

"Or how about turning on your shower and being stained purple because someone had put grape Kool-Aid powder in the showerhead?" I didn't mention that in this case it had been my trick on Mike.

Now Dr. James was laughing aloud.

He took a breath, and I slipped in my question.

"So I was wondering, sir," I said. "Would you mind helping me play a return trick on my friend?"

CHAPTER  13

Three hours later I found myself at the front door of Abe Avery's mountainside house, staring into the face of the kid who had pushed me down Kamikaze Run.

"I'm glad we could all finally get together," Abe Avery was saying from behind the kid. The old man's voice was a distant echo in my head, his words only half heard as I tried to keep from showing surprise.

What had this kid said at the top of Kamikaze Run when I told him he didn't own the ski hill? That it was only a matter of time before he did. Now it made sense—he was part of the Avery family.

Yet the kid's narrow face showed only friendliness as he confirmed my guess. "J. P. Avery. Abe is my grandfather," he said, extending a hand for me to shake.

I couldn't believe it. Here I was, slight concussion, taped-up ribs, cast on my left leg. There he was, white T-shirt and jeans, pretending that we'd never met, that he hadn't pushed me into a rocket-run of terror earlier today.

Anger filled me. Enough anger that I didn't even want to hide it.

"You're a jerk." I ignored his hand and spoke softly so that my words wouldn't reach Abe. "I was nearly killed today."

He dropped his jaw. *Surprised that I'm not prepared to play his games?*

Before he could react, voices broke through our temporary stand-off.

"Come on in, crutches or not," Abe called out, voice full of cheer. He'd already been informed of my accident. "Supper's on. And my sister will scalp me if I don't feed you right."

"Out of my way, cripple," Mike said as he elbowed me aside to push his way into the front hallway. "It's cold out here."

"Fine," I told him. "Just ignore my broken leg."

He did.

Lisa, Ralphy, and Joel followed Mike inside. They were already halfway out of their coats before I could stump in on my crutches. I barely had time to stop Joel and take his toy pistol away from him before the kid scooted away. At least Lisa was considerate enough to let me lean on her as I struggled with my own coat. J. P. Avery had disappeared into the house by the time I had straightened.

It was awkward, moving through the hallway and into the open living room, then to the kitchen, on crutches. To add to my frustration, the smell of roast turkey waiting ahead made my stomach growl. Add that to my headache and sore ribs, and it wasn't difficult to pretend I was in terrible pain from a broken leg that wasn't broken.

When I finally arrived, everyone else was seated at the table. A tall man rose to introduce himself.

"Robert Avery," he said. "Abe's son."

The explanation wasn't necessary. He had the same angular cheekbones as Abe Avery, but even as the younger and similar version, he somehow didn't seem as big or as strong as his father.

"I heard about your accident," he said as I shuffled closer to the table. His voice wasn't as deep or as confident as his father's, either. "Unfortunate, wasn't it?"

"Yes, sir," I said. "But I'm happy it wasn't worse." What I wanted to add was why it had happened. I looked over the table to glare at the cause of the accident.

Then *my* jaw fell.

There were two J. P.s.

One, in the white T-shirt, was still looking puzzled. The other, in a blue T-shirt, seemed just as startled as I was.

I felt the flush of embarrassment heat my face. No wonder J. P. had shown only friendliness. It wasn't he who had pushed me but the one in the blue T-shirt.

The other kid, his identical twin, was now squirming in his chair.

"You're—um—Ricky Kidd?" He couldn't keep the sharpness of surprise out of his voice.

Robert Avery glanced sharply at his son. "Peter, you've met Ricky before?"

"I—um—think we've probably seen each other on the hill."

"You do look very familiar," I said as dryly as possible. "But I spend most of my time on beginner runs. I can't imagine you'd ski there, would you?"

Peter was saved by a fit of coughing from Abe Avery's end of the table. I didn't move, expecting the coughing to end soon. Instead, Abe coughed harder.

A woman stood from the table. I hadn't noticed her earlier because of the shock of seeing Peter. She was Robert Avery's age, with fine features and short blond hair that contrasted nicely with her green sweater and long black skirt. She moved efficiently to a kitchen cupboard and found a small pill bottle.

Abe was still coughing when she returned to the table. She placed a pill in his mouth and handed him a nearby glass of water.

Abe shook so badly from the coughing that he was unable to bring the glass to his mouth. The woman gently hit the heel of her hand against Abe's upper back. That settled him enough to finally swallow the pill.

He wiped tears from his eyes.

"Thanks, Thelma," he said.

She smiled sweetly and changed the subject. "Let's enjoy this meal."

Abe Avery nodded and, as I sat, bowed his head to begin grace as soon as possible, as if he wanted all of us to forget the embarrassment of that prolonged coughing fit.

In contrast to the plainer cooking of the day before when just Abe had been here, this meal had extra sauces and stuffing to go with slices of turkey. Instead of just potatoes, we also had our choice of carrots and peas, or corn, or yams, or in Mike's case, lots of everything.

During the meal, I explained how a red, white, and blue hat had confused me into getting on the wrong chair lift. That, of course, drew laughter.

I explained, too, that I had underestimated the danger of Kamikaze Run and would have been much better off asking for someone to help me down. I decided not to mention how I actually had got started down the run. Peter shouldn't have pushed me, but I had led him to believe I knew what I was doing. And I was sure Peter and I would have a chance to discuss it later, especially as he seemed relieved that I was ignoring his part in the matter.

Then I explained the rope breaking on the sled.

"I'll be speaking to the ski patrol people tomorrow," Abe said with a suddenly gritted jaw. "That sort of accident is intolerable."

There were murmurs of agreement from all around the table.

As the others got up from the table to move to the living room for coffee and dessert, the thought I had in the doctor's office came back to me. *What if the breaking rope hadn't been an accident?*

Yes, Abe Avery sounded sincere. Still, I couldn't shake my doubts. Who better to know how to make a ski hill unsafe than the person who had built it? A person determined to get some insurance money?

At that moment, with only Abe and me left at the table, I was extremely aware of the weight of the cast on my leg and why that cast was there. Yes, I did want to play a couple of jokes on Mike and Ralphy, so they had no idea my leg was fine. But I had more in mind, and that's what frightened me. Especially in face-to-face conversation with the prime suspect.

So I forced my face to be still and nodded agreement with Abe Avery as he continued to explain why the ski patrol should never make mistakes.

He opened his mouth to say something else but never had a chance to finish.

"I don't believe it!" Thelma cried from the front window. "The gold miner's daughter is moving across the valley!"

CHAPTER 14

Thelma had not lied. Nor had Miss Avery's magazine article. She was there—the gold miner's daughter.

I stood at the side of the window and, along with the others, stared down the mountainside at what the moonlight showed so clearly.

It was a young woman, with the length of a football field between her and Abe's cabin. She was too far away for us to see the details of her face but close enough that we could see the hood over her head and the gray-shrouded clothing that loosely covered her body. Close enough to be able to see the lantern that she awkwardly held high with her left hand.

"I don't believe this," Mike blurted.

With ten of us crowded at the window, it was still so quiet that I heard someone softly draw a breath to reply. But the words were not spoken.

Because the figure walked right through a tree.

Until then, I had been prepared to believe that the ghost was anything but a ghost. A skilled actress, maybe. Someone playing a practical joke. But not truly a ghost.

Now I felt my knees go weak.

The moonlight was silver, strong enough to cast shadows among the trees where she walked. Strong enough so that I couldn't blame darkness for creating an illusion.

The figure paused and looked back, as if someone had

called her name.

Then it walked through another tree.

These were trees with thick trunks, bare at the base so that the overhang of branches that drooped from the weight of the snow formed a canopy like a giant umbrella.

And the figure had walked beneath the canopy and without pausing had walked directly through the base of the tree.

The gray shrouds and high-held lantern didn't even flicker. They were visible on the approach to the tree and visible on the other side and didn't flow around or even flicker as the figure moved through the tree.

I heard someone moan.

It was me.

Then I realized something and I wanted to faint.

"No shadow," I whispered. "She casts no shadow."

Which was too true. The figure continued to glide forward. Again she stopped and turned her head as if someone had called. And every single second of her ghostly journey, she passed among the tree shadows so sharply outlined on the smooth snow, yet she cast no shadow herself.

"I want to throw up," Ralphy said.

So did I.

But I couldn't take my eyes off the figure. She stopped and turned one last time in the identical manner as the first two turns, took several more steps, then disappeared.

She didn't move behind a tree. Didn't run away. Just disappeared. There one second, gone the next.

"Tell me that all of you saw that," Lisa said in hushed tones. "Otherwise I'll think I've gone crazy."

The room broke into excited murmurings as we all agreed with her. If the others were like me, it was all one-sided conversation. My mouth was moving and my lips were speaking, but I wasn't hearing anything said in return. It was like we would all burst unless we were trying to explain what had happened, even if no one was listening because everyone was trying to explain in return.

The babble rose.

And one more thought froze me into silence.

"Mike," I hissed. "Come here!"

He moved toward me in small, stunned steps. His eyes were still wide, and the whiteness of his face made his freckles seem to glow.

"I . . . it wasn't . . . it couldn't . . . it . . ."

"I saw the same thing, Mike," I assured him. "But I need your legs right now."

"Sure," he said. "Chop them off."

It was good to see color return to his face. A sick joke like that meant he was coming back to normal. There wasn't time to laugh, though. My thoughts were too urgent.

I grabbed his arm and spoke. "I mean I need you to put your boots on and check something out."

He stared at me.

"No shadow," I told him. "But did she leave footprints?"

He stared longer as my words sank in.

"Don't say to me what I think you're going to say to me," he pleaded.

"I have to," I said. "I can't do it myself. Someone's got to check to see if the gold miner's daughter left footprints in the snow. Now, before wind or a storm or people move through the area."

"But it might—"

"What could a ghost do?" I asked. "It wasn't even solid enough to—"

I stopped as I realized what I was saying.

"—to bounce off a tree," Mike finished. "And you want me out there in the darkness looking for it."

"Not for it," I said. "For footprints. Anything to prove it wasn't what we thought it was."

"But—"

I stooped to a desperate level. "Not chicken, are you, Mike? Because I could always ask Lisa."

He glared at me. "Jerk. I can't believe you'd use that line on me."

I smiled. "Your boots are in the front hall. Slip out now and you'll be back in two minutes."

Trouble was, Mike didn't find any footprints.

Even more troubling was the question that Lisa asked.

"If the ghost appears as a warning," she said when Mike reported his findings in the living room a few minutes later, "what accident will happen tomorrow?"

CHAPTER 15

The next morning I woke up knowing that there were only six days of Colorado vacation left and that for a normal person with a leg in a cast, there was very little to do at a mountain resort. No skiing, no swimming in the indoor pool, no nothing.

Mike and Ralphy, however, often accuse me of not being normal. In this case, they were right. I had two things to do.

One was to get to the hospital and back. Two was to examine the ski patrol sled.

Task number one was easy. Ralphy, Mike, Lisa, and Joel hit the ski slopes immediately after breakfast. That left me alone to catch the shuttle bus back toward Colorado Springs. From a shuttle bus drop off, I took a cab to the hospital.

"Tough break, huh?" the cab driver grinned as I fumbled my way into the backseat and placed my crutches across my legs. "Get it? Break?"

"If you only knew, sir," I said. The cast and crutches were so difficult to maneuver that I couldn't imagine how much worse it would be if I were also suffering the pain of a broken bone.

I gave him my destination and we were there within minutes.

During my time in the waiting room, I replayed the previous evening's ghostly visit again and again. Not only because it was so weird, but because something was bothering me about the ghost, something that I couldn't quite bring to the front of my mind.

Dr. James interrupted my thoughts a few minutes later and escorted me into a small room.

It was like most hospital examining rooms, with various gadgets and rubber tubes, but with a small difference. A saw with a round, toothless blade lay on the counter. A plastic garbage can below was filled with pieces of broken plaster.

"Normally one of our aides does this," Dr. James said. "But because we're keeping this one a secret between you and me, I thought I'd do it myself. The less people who know, the better. Right?"

He winked at me. "Plus it doesn't have to reach the billing statement."

"That's very kind of you, sir, but—"

He put up his hands to silence me. "No buts. We made our deal yesterday. I help you with your joke, and you write later to tell me all about it."

I sincerely hoped that the promised letter would just be filled with fun and games. Thinking of the ghost, however, led to serious doubts. I shivered.

Dr. James noticed that shiver and placed his hand on my forehead. "Do you feel okay?"

"Yes," I said. "It's nothing."

Physically I did feel fine. The slight concussion, as Dr. James had promised, had left me with only a slight headache. As long as I didn't twist or stretch suddenly, my ribs didn't stab me with pain. And, of course, except for some itchiness inside the cast, my leg was okay.

"Glad to hear it," Dr. James said. "Now let's get down to work. It's bad enough you had to make an extra trip in today because the cast needed time to harden."

He set me on an examining bench with my legs resting straight out in front of me. Then he grabbed the saw and flicked a switch.

A loud screeching whine filled the room.

He flicked it off again. "It's only the noise that's frightening," Dr.

James said. "This blade is designed to cut through only hard material. It can't break skin. You might feel some warmth, but you'll be fine."

I nodded.

Dr. James put a mask over his mouth, started the saw, and cut a line down the left side of my cast. Plaster dust rose as the blade bit through, and I coughed.

My mind wandered back to Abe Avery and his coughing. It reminded me that in the excitement of the ghost sighting, I'd forgotten some unanswered questions from last night's supper.

Thelma had just been introduced as Thelma. But I had seen no wedding ring on her left hand. If she wasn't married, was she there as a date for Robert Avery? If she was a date, where was Robert's wife, the mother of J. P. and Peter? If Thelma wasn't a date, what was she doing there? Did it have anything to do with the competent way she had helped Abe Avery with his coughing fit? Maybe the best way to find out would be to speak to Peter. . . .

"What's that?" Dr. James asked.

"Um, nothing, sir." Deep in my thoughts, I'd barely realized I was mumbling out loud.

Dr. James nodded, then began cutting a line down the other side of my cast.

At least this is working, I thought. When we finished, I'd have a tiny advantage on whoever was creating the accidents at Zebulon. I'd have a cast on my leg, which gave me the excuse not to be skiing. But I'd have a cast that I could remove at any time, which gave me the freedom to wander about if I kept my face hidden—something easy to do at a ski resort where it wasn't unusual to wear ski goggles and a hat.

The halves of the cast fell away from my leg.

"Perfect," Dr. James said. He reached into his pocket and pulled out some giant rubber bands the same color as my cast. "These will keep the cast around your leg. Your friend will never guess who's playing the tricks on him."

I smiled. "It'll definitely be a surprise."

It was definitely a surprise to walk into the waiting room ahead of Dr. James and discover that Abe Avery was leaning back in one of the chairs, a magazine held in his hand, and his eyes staring at a spot on the far wall.

"Mr. Avery," I said. I felt instant nervousness, as if he had known exactly what I was doing and why.

He shifted his eyes to me and, for a second, didn't seem to realize I was there.

"Oh," he said finally, "it's you, Ricky."

His heavy tone told me that he was not here because of me. I relaxed slightly.

"You know this young man, Abe?" Dr. James said.

"Sure, Doc," Abe replied. "He's a friend of my sister."

Dr. James and Abe know each other?

It must have been a logical question to ask myself, because Dr. James gave an immediate explanation.

"Abe and I go way back," Dr. James said. "As one of the only doctors between—"

"—Zebulon and Colorado Springs," Abe interrupted, "and as one of the oldest doctors around, he—"

"I've put him together more times than a cat has kittens," Dr. James finished with a smile.

"You sure have," Abe said, a smile lighting his own eyes briefly. "For how many years now? Forty—"

He didn't finish, because coughing took him again.

Dr. James helped him stand.

Abe found his breath long enough to speak to me. "Ricky, wait around. I'll give you a ride back."

I nodded.

Abe and Dr. James returned ten minutes later. They were sadly quiet, and Abe remained in a silence that I sensed should not be broken.

We were halfway to Zebulon in Abe's Jeep before I discovered the reason for that silence.

"Beautiful mountains, aren't they, son?"

"Yes, sir," I said. Sunlight carved deep shadows among the ridges of the towering granite. Patches of brilliant white cloud clung to sharp peaks. The road ahead of us twisted and rose to disappear and reappear throughout the deep valleys.

"Mountains can make a man feel small and big at the same time."

"Sir?"

He didn't take his eyes off the road. I think he was talking more to himself than to me. "Small because you realize how puny you are compared to the powers of God and nature."

He smiled to himself. "Big, because it makes you bust inside with an ache of freedom that I can't explain even after a lifetime here. Like maybe your soul is instinctively trying to reach for God, even as your body holds you here to earth."

"I think I understand, sir." I remembered the vastness of the wide open plains during a bus ride from Jamesville to Montana and how all that sky and horizon had made me want to soar like the hawks that rode the wind-draft columns of heated air. "In fact, I know I understand."

More silence.

Then, miles later, Abe spoke again. Softly.

"I'll miss these mountains indeed," he said. "But much as it will hurt to miss them, I'm glad I had a life among them."

He chuckled. "Just like when Myrtle, my wife, bless her departed soul, left me behind a few years back. Much as it hurt, I wouldn't have traded our memories for the world."

I knew I shouldn't say anything.

He finally turned to me.

"Son, live life as hard and as well as you can. It's a gift from God."

I thought of his coughing fits, and I hoped I was wrong in my understanding of what he meant or why he was saying it.

I wasn't.

"I've been able to beat everything else," he said as explanation. "But now the cancer is winning."

"Cancer?"

Surprise crossed his face. "I thought my sister would have told you."

I shook my head.

"Then I'm sorry to have burdened you," he said.

"No burden, sir." He was so simple and direct that it didn't feel uncomfortable like it had in the hospital with Miss Avery when I had wanted to pretend everything was fine. Instead, I felt and shared his sadness but at the same time took strength from his strength.

"At least I've got time to straighten my affairs," he said. The road hummed beneath us during the next few seconds as he waited to speak again. "Doc James has scheduled me to go into the hospital in two weeks. He thinks I'll be gone before spring."

I thought I could ask, so I did. "Aren't you afraid?"

He took his eyes off the road briefly and smiled sadly at me. "I'd be lying if I told you I was looking forward to it."

He watched the road again. "But afraid? No."

He thought a moment. "Son, no matter who you are, there's one question you've got to decide. Is God real? Century after century, it's the most complex question that mankind has faced.

"Every person in every generation has to make their own decision, no matter what the greatest men and women of previous generations have said. Our generation? It seems we're the first to want to pretend the question doesn't exist. Even if the answer is no, and I'm certainly not saying it's no, but even if the answer was no, it's still something you gotta ask. Somehow our televisions, newspapers, radios, and movies avoid even bringing the subject up. Still—"

He took another quick glance to see if I was listening.

I was.

"Still, you gotta decide. Some folks decide no. Some folks don't decide, which is just the same as no. And others take a small leap of faith, then discover how much everything on earth points to a God of love. Even with all the pain in our world, it makes life worth living."

He gave me another smile. "My answer? My heart tells me yes. I know my life is part of something much greater than me. That makes it easier to look beyond."

He tapped the steering wheel. "In fact, my biggest worry is what may happen to my family if the resort goes."

CHAPTER 16

"Abe's not afraid to die?" Mike asked me.

Five hours had passed since Abe dropped me off in front of our resort building and continued up the narrow road to his own house perched on the side of the hill.

"No," I told Mike. I stared past him out the window of the restaurant as I retold Abe's words.

Our table, now half-covered with Mike's gloves, hat, ski goggles, and scarf, stood beside the window. It was late afternoon and the sun had already set behind the mountain on the western half of the valley. A few skiers were straggling down the hills, and the remaining light gave a view of the opposite mountainside above us and of the resort buildings slightly below. A sprinkling of fresh snow the night before had covered most of the soot from the burned building at the far end of the resort, so there was nothing to mar the beauty of the view.

Except for my own thoughts. Thoughts of the sadness of good-byes at the end of life. And thoughts of deliberate accidents adding to that sadness.

"Come on," Mike said. "Look this way. This is me. You know, the great Mike Andrews? Guaranteed to brighten your day and make your life miserable?"

With effort, I took my eyes away from a lazy, unfocused staring in the distance and looked at Mike.

He had one eyebrow raised, his tongue out and waggling back and forth, and a hand on each side of his head as he pulled his ears outward.

I managed a half-laugh of affection and resignation at the tactics designed to cheer me up.

"Okay," I said. "I get the hint."

I took a deep breath.

"I haven't had a chance to talk to you much," I said. "When you haven't been out on the slopes, things have been too crazy—"

"Like a ghost I don't want to believe I saw."

"Exactly. Or when we've been in our hotel room, I haven't wanted to discuss much of my thoughts because you can't predict what Joel might do with what he hears us say."

Mike nodded.

"So anyway, I'd been thinking that maybe Abe Avery was behind the fire and some of the other things."

"What? He owns the resort!"

I explained my insurance theory to Mike.

"Makes sense," Mike finally agreed.

"But not anymore," I said. "Now I just can't see Abe doing something like this. He's known about the cancer for a while. Why would he wreck the resort it took years to build up, just to collect money that he won't live long enough to spend?"

It also rid me of my private fear that Joel might be in danger.

"That makes sense, too," Mike said. "So you're back to square one."

"Which consists of a ghost and too many accidents."

I explained to Mike what I'd heard from the ambulance guy and from Dr. James.

"Accidents like broken legs," Mike said, pointing sympathetically to my own leg and cast that was propped on a chair beside our table.

"That's, um, the other thing," I said.

Somehow practical jokes seemed trivial after spending that quiet, sad time in Abe's Jeep with him. Now the only reason I wanted to be thought of as injured was for the freedom my "broken leg" would give me in searching the resort. Freedom I'd already taken advantage of earlier.

"Mike, I don't have a broken leg."

"Sure, pal. You're giving up all the time on the ski slopes because you figure staying in the room and reading books is more fun." He thought about that for a second and grinned. "Actually, that's probably close to the truth. You and Ralphy are the biggest bookworm geeks that I know."

"Mike, I don't have a broken leg."

He stared at me. "You're serious, aren't you?"

I told him why and what I hoped to do.

"Cool," Mike said. "You're in disguise looking for clues, and our job is to ski every day and pretend that everything is normal? It's a rough job—"

"—but someone's got to do it," I finished for him. It felt good to have even a half-smile on my face. Especially because of what I'd found earlier while taking advantage of the freedom of a non-broken leg.

"Mike, when do you expect the others to get back?"

"Soon," he said. "They were going to try an intermediate run. So they took the last chair up the hill."

"Joel too?"

"You should see him. The kid's a whiz on skis. Of course, he looked goofy today because he insisted on putting his cowboy hat on."

I shook my head. Some skiers actually did wear cowboy hats. The rebel image, I guess. Once Joel had spotted one of them, there was no stopping him from wearing his own hat. It had been major work getting him not to carry his toy gun with him.

"Maybe when they get back, we can send Joel to the room to watch the cartoon channel and you, me, Lisa, and Ralphy can brainstorm here."

"Sure," Mike said. "Any hints now?"

"Unfortunately, yes."

"Fire when ready."

"When I got back from the hospital, I left my cast in the room and bundled up my face with a scarf and goggles and did a little research. I tracked down the wrecked toboggan sled behind the ski patrol office."

"And?"

"And I'm lucky the sled took most of the impact for me. It was mangled but good."

"And?" Mike repeated. "I can see some of that Ricky Kidd anger building in your face."

"And the rope had not broken by accident. The rope had broken on each side, just at the knots that attached each side to the sled. A break on just one side would mean that the ski patrol would have at least had one tow line to the sled. But a break on both sides meant that the ski patrol was left with short pieces of rope in their hands and a runaway sled."

I took another breath.

"Mike, both breaks were clean. As if someone had used a knife to cut three-quarters of the way through and let the weight of a person snap the rest."

"You could have been killed."

His statement said it all. If not me, the next person to be in that sled. Or the person after.

I began to say something to that effect.

Thunder stopped me.

Thunder? But this is winter.

Sudden movement caught my eyes. Again I looked past Mike and out the restaurant window into the fading light.

The thunder grew. As did a gigantic plume of white rising high above the trees.

Mike half turned in his chair to see what had silenced me.

The plume rose and churned and flowed like a monstrous river and coursed down the mountainside. Trees snapped in its path, pushed aside as effortlessly as if a fire hose had been turned on straw.

Any skiers still out there will be buried in tons of snow. And Lisa and Ralphy and Joel—

"The ghost," Mike managed to say. "A warning last night for this—"

"Don't say it," I told him. "Please don't say it."

He said it anyway. Grimly and with horror.

"Avalanche."

CHAPTER 17

Eternity lasted one hour. That's how long it took for us to hear the click of the key card in the door of our hotel room.

Ralphy walked in, whistling, followed by Joel in his cowboy hat.

I stopped pacing and almost leaped forward to give them each a hug. They weren't dead!

"Hey, guys, what's up?" Ralphy said. "I'm hungry."

"Ricky," Joel said, "can I have my gun back?"

What?

Here I'd spent the last hour convinced they had died in the avalanche, and now they were just strolling in, cheerful and unconcerned.

"What's up?" I said, suddenly angry. "What's up? Your funeral, that's what. Mike and I were going crazy."

Ralphy's eyes bugged out at my response. Joel merely marched over to the desk where I thought I'd so carefully hidden his toy revolver and pulled it out.

"Yeah," Mike chimed in with equal anger from the bed where he had sat the entire hour with his head bowed. "We were worried to death about you guys. You never called. Nothing."

"But, but—" Ralphy began.

He didn't have a chance to finish. Mike and I caught each other's glances and started to laugh.

"I can't believe I said that," Mike said. "I sounded just like my mother."

I groaned agreement. Joel and his gun and his cowboy hat took the opportunity to edge away from all of us.

"Sorry, Ralpho," I said. "We saw the avalanche from the restaurant, and the longer it took for you to get here, the more we knew you'd been buried in it."

I then called through the now empty doorway so that my voice would carry into the hall. "Joel, I took the caps out."

A roll of caps was now in my ski jacket pocket, where they'd stay for a while. Resorts weren't good places for Joel to be shooting bandits or cattle rustlers.

Ralphy pulled his ski hat off his head. He's the only guy I know whose hair looks neater after wearing one than before.

"It didn't even cross my mind that you'd worry about us," Ralphy apologized. "I just assumed you knew it happened on the far slopes."

"We did," Mike said, still with a trace of impatience. "Ricky already told you we saw it from the restaurant."

Ralphy kept speaking as he peeled out of his ski suit. "Well, the chair lift for the far slopes closes a half hour earlier than the other hills. That gives the ski patrol a head start on sweeping the far runs for stragglers. There was no chance that *anyone* got buried in the avalanche."

Mike snapped his jaw shut.

"We knew that," I said. "Mike was just testing you."

"Glad I passed," Ralphy said. Sometimes he misses sarcasm.

"So what took you so long?" I asked. "If you're hungry, I guess you didn't stop for a bite to eat."

"Ran into J. P. Avery," Ralphy replied. "We got to talking about the avalanche and other things."

"Other things?" Mike echoed. "Don't tell me he reads encyclopedias in his spare time, too."

Ralphy shook his head no. "I haven't forgotten why Miss Avery sent us here, you know: so we could be her eyes and ears. So all day I've been thinking about what hadn't been mentioned in the letter."

"The ghosts and the accidents," Mike said.

"And Thelma," Ralphy said. "The letter mentioned that everyone was fine. It included everyone's name, except for Thelma's."

I grinned delight. "I've been thinking the same, Ralphy. Like, is she married to Robert, is she his girlfriend, or what?"

"Well, J. P.'s real mom died in a car accident when they were really young. And he's guessing that Thelma might be a stepmom sometime in the next year."

"That's case-breaking news," Mike said.

Ralphy rolled his eyeballs. "No, it's not. It's background info. Like now knowing that Thelma is a nurse, who met the Avery family while she was helping Abe. But J. P. didn't want to talk about it that much."

"Ralphy," I said as gently as possible, "Abe has lung cancer."

We all thought about that in silence for a while.

I tried to break the mood. "So, Ralpho, what else did you get for background?"

"J. P.'s dad—"

"Robert," Mike added.

"Robert is some sort of expert on lasers. You know, light amplification by stimulated emission of radiation."

"Thanks, Einstein," Mike said. "We knew that."

Ralphy sailed on, unhurt by Mike's mild sarcasm. "Robert had some job with the military in Colorado Springs but moved here about a year ago to learn how to run the resort. Again, J. P. bounced around the subject of why."

"That would make sense," Mike said. "Maybe it was about a year ago that Abe discovered he had . . . well, you know."

We nodded.

"So if they all knew that Robert would be inheriting this resort, maybe it seemed like a good idea to learn how to run it before he takes it over."

"I could go along with that," Ralphy said. "J. P. and Peter are here to stay. They don't even leave the resort to go to school."

"Cool," Mike said. "Ski, ski, ski."

"Nope. Homeschooling." Ralphy paused a second. "I think Thelma helps out with that now, too."

Something was bothering me, but I couldn't figure out what. Something about the move from Colorado Springs.

"Earth to Ricky," I heard Mike say. "Earth calling Ricky Kidd."

"Very funny," I said.

"Not as funny as starving to death. Isn't it time we called Lisa and started thinking about supper?"

"Yup. You guys go on ahead," I said. "I'll look for Joel."

I didn't have to look long. Only thirty seconds after Ralphy and Mike left, Joel found me.

He skidded into the room, eyes wide. "There's another alarm clock!"

I started to sigh. Then the significance of one word hit me. *Another.* As in one like before. And before when he said he'd seen an alarm clock—

"Show me," I said.

He ran out again. I followed him at full speed on my crutches to the end of the hallway, then up the stairs and down that hallway to a door marked "Laundry Room."

Joel pointed to the shut door.

What had he said at supper the first night at Abe's? *"The fire chased me from the towels and alarm clock."*

I sniffed.

Gasoline! The dark carpet was stained slightly darker with a line that ran all the way down the hallway.

It wasn't difficult to put together. A timer inside the laundry room set to ignite a trail of gasoline. *Towels and alarm clock.*

But the next question might be the killer. Literally. *When would the timer go off?*

I could run now. But would that give us enough time to clear the building? And even if no one was hurt, there'd still be another gigantic fire.

Or I could open the door and pray there was still enough time left on the timer and that I'd know how to disconnect it if there was.

"Beat it, Joel," I said. "Get back to the room. Put your coat on and then wait for me outside."

Joel caught the urgency in my voice and, for a change, actually listened.

I turned the handle of the door, opened it slowly, and almost gagged at the suddenly overpowering smell of gasoline.

There it was.

In the half-light of the laundry room, I saw the glowing red numbers of a digital alarm clock.

11:58:21.

But it was nearly six o'clock. That didn't make sense. Unless this was set to go off at a convenient time on the clock, like at 12:00.

11:58:31.

Which would mean I had barely more than a minute to figure out how to disconnect all of this. And the towels were soaked with gasoline.

11:58:42.

Wires led from the alarm clock to a tiny lump of dough just beneath the towels. *Think! Think! Think!*

11:59:07.

Did I dare touch those wires? What if that short-circuited something? Gasoline vapors literally explode at contact with a spark, and I was standing in a near puddle of it in a small, enclosed area.

11:59:15.

There was only one thing I could think of doing.

I unplugged the alarm clock and scrambled backward.

Nothing happened. No explosion of light. No roar of flame.

And the alarm clock no longer glowed those deadly red electronic numbers.

"Hey, punk," an adult voice said behind me. "What do you think you're doing in there?"

I turned to see a fat, unshaven man in a bathrobe walking down the hallway toward me—bottle of beer in one hand, an unlit cigarette in the other.

"That's right. You."

I was speechless.

"Making noise and clunking up and down the hallway with those stupid crutches. How's a guy supposed to grab a snooze around here?"

I still said nothing. My heart was pounding too badly, and the sweat on my forehead felt like squeezed out blood.

"Kids nowadays," the fat man snorted. "I'll learn you respect."

He placed the unlit cigarette in his mouth and took a lighter out of his pocket as he moved closer.

"Don't!" I shouted. The gasoline vapors were all around from the now open laundry room.

"Punk," he said. He bent his head forward and lifted the lighter to his mouth.

I didn't even feel bad as I slammed his hand with the end of my crutch.

Later, I told myself as he howled with pain, later I would have a chance to explain how bad smoking would be for his health.

CHAPTER 18

"If I could afford it, son," Abe Avery told me the next morning, "I'd give you ten thousand dollars."

His smile was weak and barely displaced the haunted look which had filled his face last night to see for himself the alarm clock and rigged gasoline bomb in the laundry room.

It was obvious that the passing of the night had not eased his troubles. Abe's smile was brief, and the look of haunted pain settled again on his face.

"Ten thousand is a lot of money, sir."

"Not near as much as you and your brother saved me. So a typewriter is the least I can do for you today. But why a typewriter instead of a computer? I thought only people from my generation used those things."

At ten in the morning, with the kettle whistling in the kitchen behind us, and with cups and saucers on a low table gleaming in sunlight that streamed through the large picture window into the living room where we sat, it seemed unreal that a ghost had recently walked the hillside below among moonlit shadows, that someone had tried burning yet another resort building, that an avalanche had wiped out the upper part of a chair lift on the far slopes.

Yet a quick glance at Abe's thoughtful stare out the same window showed all of the troubles were too real.

"Thelma, would it be much trouble for you to round up a

typewriter in the next while?" Abe called to the kitchen.

"None," Thelma replied. She was already halfway into the living room, carrying a large pot of tea. "Why does our heroic invalid need a typewriter? Why not a computer?"

I tried not to blush. Thelma was very pretty, and she had added a mysterious smile to her compliment.

"I just asked him that," Abe said.

"Um, a school essay," I said. Which was true. I did need to get started. "I thought since I'm not skiing, I might as well do something. With a typewriter, I don't need to worry about whether the power goes out. There have been some outages lately and . . ."

"I know what you mean," she said. "When the power goes off, you can lose everything that wasn't saved."

I nodded.

Thelma smiled again, a smile that made me feel as if I'd just informed her that I'd climbed Mount Everest.

Thelma lifted the teapot by the wire handle and began to try to pour. She set it down again.

"Abe—"

He lifted the teapot and poured for her.

"An old skiing accident," Thelma explained as she rubbed her left wrist. "These bones have never been the same."

She sat beside me and touched my cast. "Let's hope the same doesn't happen to you."

"I'm not losing sleep about it," I said. It was very tempting to tell those deep green eyes the truth about my cast. Fortunately a knock at the door interrupted me.

Abe raised his eyebrows.

"You're feeling poorly," Thelma said. "I'll get it."

She rose and moved to the door. She opened it, and beyond her shoulders, we could see that the man at the door wore a green parka, work clothes that identified him as one of the Zebulon resort employees.

He said a few words in low tones.

Thelma looked back over her shoulder at Abe, turned back to the man, shook her head a few times, and said a few more words to end the conversation.

The man nodded, then left.

Thelma returned in quiet seriousness. "Abe," she said, "no sense in trying to break this gently. Yesterday's avalanche was no accident."

Abe's knuckles whitened where he held the cup of tea. I wondered if the china would shatter, so intense was the anger that crossed his face.

"How does he know?" Abe asked. His question was voiced not with doubt but with resignation.

"He says they found traces of dynamite at the top of the mountain."

Thelma turned to me. "It's common to use dynamite to trigger small avalanches in danger areas near the boundaries of the ski areas. But never..."

"Never above a ski run," Abe said. "I can only imagine the results if this had happened during the day instead of when the far slopes were cleared. It'd be enough to finally force us into bankruptcy."

He set his cup down. "I'm sorry to have to ask you this, Ricky. But can you keep this news to yourself?"

I didn't reply soon enough for him. My mind was thinking of the gasoline and alarm clock and the fact that then, too, Abe had insisted that the police not be called.

"I'll explain," he sighed, as if he felt my short silence meant I would not keep the news to myself. "It has to do with a buyout."

"Sir?"

"When Dr. James discovered my illness, it seemed like a good idea to plan ahead. My son, Robert, moved here to learn how to run the resort. After all, it would be his soon enough. But Robert doesn't enjoy his job as general manager of the ski resort. And we've had our share of troubles. So it seemed wisest to try to sell the resort."

I nodded.

"We have an interested buyer," Abe continued. "A group of Japanese businessmen who have been looking things over since about August. Good thing, too. Things have been bad lately, and if Zebulon doesn't sell to someone who has the money to turn it around, it won't be around next season. I lose a lifetime of work, and Robert and my grandchildren lose their inheritance."

Abe stared out the window. "I'm afraid that too much more bad news will scare away our interested buyers. I want a chance to straighten this out before it sells."

Thelma moved behind Abe and dropped a comforting hand on his shoulder.

"Ricky," Abe said, "negotiations have been moving quickly. The Japanese businessmen arrive today to make their final offer. Anything might scare them off or, at best, cause them to lower the price. And inheritance tax is going to take enough as it is."

He read correctly the hesitation in my eyes. "It's not dishonest," he said. "I'll get to the bottom of these accidents, and then the resort will be worth whatever price is agreed upon today."

Now his broad hands were twisting slightly in his lap. I imagined the anguish he must feel, and his worries. It was not difficult to promise I would keep it to myself.

"Thank you," he said with dignity. "As soon as a price is settled, I'll call in the authorities."

He reached for his cup of tea, then stopped.

"Oh yes," he said to me. "Your typewriter."

"If you'll trust me with it, that would be great," I said. "I'll have it back to you by tomorrow afternoon."

"I'd gladly trust you with it," Abe said, "but I don't have one."

Now why did I assume he had one? It's not like one has been in plain sight in his house over the last few visits.

"I'll check the front desk to see if they have one somewhere in storage," Thelma said, "then arrange for it to be sent to his room."

She looked at her watch. "I should do it soon, too. Our appointment with the buyers is less than a half hour away."

"That's a hint, isn't it?" I heard my voice saying. But my mind was elsewhere. Because I knew why I'd made the assumption about the typewriter. And my mouth kept moving in automatic gear. "So I guess I should go now."

I remembered the time in Miss Avery's hospital room. I could see clearly the letter I'd read aloud. The letter with the faded type, as if the typewriter ribbon was very old.

If Abe doesn't have a typewriter, who wrote the letter to Miss Avery?

CHAPTER  19

Who was the bad guy?

And why?

Or maybe if I figured out the why, then I'd figure out the bad guy.

Those thoughts, and the itchiness of my leg beneath the cast, were nearly enough to send me to the top of Kamikaze Run again, this time to ski down with my eyes closed and hope for the worst.

The cast, at least, was something I could control. So I hobbled back to our hotel room, locked the door behind me, and removed the rubber bands that held both halves of the cast in place. Then I flexed and stretched my leg.

Eleven in the morning, the alarm clock on the table beside the bed told me.

Everyone else was skiing and probably wouldn't come down from the slopes until midafternoon. I was too restless to read any of my books. That left me hours to kill, but with no idea how to kill them, no idea where to start looking or what to look for.

I lay back on the bed and stared at the ceiling.

The stupid light was too bright.

I got up, flicked the light switch, and lay back down again.

Five past eleven, the digital numbers on the clock read.

Even if the typewriter arrived soon, I'd spend only an hour on my essay. What I really wanted to do was answer some of Miss Avery's questions.

But where to start? What good did it do to have the fake cast when I had nowhere to go?

I closed my eyes.

Who is the bad guy? And why?

What did I have so far? Not much.

One, Abe Avery did not have a typewriter. The letter that reached Miss Avery had been typewritten.

Two, the ghost and the accidents had not been mentioned in Miss Avery's letter. A ghost and accidents definitely were happening. These were things Abe would have put into a letter.

Easy conclusion—Abe Avery had not written the letter that Miss Avery showed us in Jamesville.

Then there was Abe's surprise that Miss Avery had not told me about his cancer. Surprise because he assumed that she knew. But what if this was something else that had been left out of the fake letters, something that Miss Avery did not know?

Aaaargh! Think, Ricky Kidd, think.

11:09:30.

Okay, I asked myself with a sigh, what conclusions could I draw from the fact that someone had been sending fake letters to Miss Avery?

I remembered a class project where we wrote our own newspaper. The teacher had drilled into us the "Five *W*s." What? Where? When? Who? Why?

So if the letter was my only clue, I should apply What, Where, When, Who, Why.

What?—I already knew. The fake letter.

Where?—from here at Zebulon all the way to Jamesville.

When? That answer didn't fall into place too easily. I struggled to remember the magazine article. It had reported that the ghost made its first appearance about . . . about a year ago. Okay, Abe should have mentioned the ghost then. Did that mean Miss Avery had been receiving fake letters for about a year?

Why? I thought hard. *Who?* Still nothing. Plus, something else was bugging me, tickling the back of my mind like a pesky fly.

11:13:25.

Why? Who? Nuts. l was still back to those questions, about both the bad guy and about the fake-letter writer.

Then I sat up and groaned.

Pretty obvious, doughhead, I told myself.

If one wasn't the other, there still must be a pretty strong connection between the bad guy and the fake-letter writer.

Then I grinned to myself.

It'd be easier to track down the fake-letter writer than it would be to track down the bad guy. And when we had the fake-letter writer, we'd probably have the bad guy.

11:15:48.

I stood up and started pacing.

Okay. Okay. Okay.

Abe thought all his letters had reached Miss Avery. That's why he was surprised that I didn't know about the cancer. Which would mean he had been writing letters but someone had been replacing them between Zebulon and Jamesville.

Who was in a position to steal his letters and put the fake ones in the mail? A resort worker? Local postman? Mail sorter? To answer that, I'd have to learn how things were usually mailed here.

Once I'd tracked down the possible *Who*s, then maybe I could start guessing at the *Why*s.

Why, of course, would leave only finding explanations for the ghost, an odd avalanche or two. Minor details like that. *Aaaargh!*

I gave my head a shake.

Concentrate on the smaller task. Unravel it from there.

Okay. Okay. Okay.

11:20:03.

First step. Put the cast back on and hobble down to the main resort building and the souvenir shop.

Second step. Buy a postcard and stamps.

Third step. Ask where to mail it.

Fourth step. Ask more questions about mailing.

I worked the cast back into place, slipped into my ski pants and jacket, grabbed my crutches, and hopped to the door.

I paused with the door half open and glanced back for a final check of the time.

Then I realized what had been the pesky fly in the back of my mind.

The red digital numbers of the alarm clock.

I closed my eyes and remembered the heart-stopping panic as I stood in the gasoline-soaked laundry room. Red digital numbers of the alarm clock.

Identical.

I opened my eyes again.

Yes. The alarm clock used for the gasoline bomb was identical to the one in our hotel room.

That meant one of three things. One, it was a coincidence. Two, the bomb clock had been stolen from a hotel room. Or three, the bomb clock had been purchased along with all the others used in the hundreds of rooms at the resort and was a spare.

Probably not a coincidence. I also doubted that someone smart enough to cause all the accidents undetected would risk getting caught in a simple theft. So if I assumed it was number three, that the bomb clock had been taken from the spares, it might mean that only someone higher up in the resort management had access to spare equipment.

That same someone, then, would also have had access to Abe Avery's mail ever since the accidents started happening.

And—I snapped my fingers—it meant that the same someone had free access to dynamite for the avalanche, free access to the toboggan sled to cut the rope, and free access to all the different ways to cause all the various accidents.

I closed the door.

Who is that one person?

I hobbled down the hallway and out the far door.

Halfway across the parking lot, I noticed a limousine move slowly to the road that led up to Abe Avery's house.

I looked closer, curious to see if it carried the Japanese businessmen.

It did. I saw at least three, each excitedly pointing in different directions as they checked out different parts of the resort.

As the limo made its turn, sunlight bounced off the side mirror and hit me directly in the eyes.

I blinked and rubbed away the pain of that sudden concentrated beam.

A concentrated beam of light!

Then I smiled. What had Ralphy said last summer about the amazing properties of concentrated light and 3-D postcards? What had he told us during background information? *Light amplification by stimulated emission of radiation.*

And what had Mike said seconds later? *Earth to Ricky. Earth calling Ricky Kidd.*

He said that because my mind was on the Averys' move from Colorado Springs to Zebulon.

Put the two together and . . .

It was a long shot but better than nothing.

My next step was no longer to buy a postcard. Instead, it was to find a pay phone and make a call back to Jamesville, where someone owed me a favor.

"Operator," I found myself saying a few minutes later, "I'd like directory assistance please—I need the number for State Trooper John Boyd."

CHAPTER 20

"So, who picks up Abe Avery's mail?" I asked Ralphy that night as we sat in the lounge area of the main resort building.

"J. P. does," he said. "What's with this meeting?"

Rats. There went my theory in one big whoosh.

"Are you sure?"

"Positive. I was asking J. P. himself. He had no reason to lie. And don't you think he'd remember if it was him?"

I sighed. Hours of careful thought and what-ifs, all lost. My own phone call didn't really prove anything on its own, and I had pinned everything on the beam of sunlight and the fact that Abe's mailing was done by—

"What's with this meeting?" Ralphy repeated.

"Probably nothing now," I said. "Depends on Lisa and Mike."

"I got through," Lisa said.

"Okay," I said. Until Ralphy had deflated me, that would have been good news. "What did your lawyer uncle have to say when you finally reached him?"

"He said, 'Hello, darling, how's the most beautiful girl in the world?' " Lisa grinned.

Mike interrupted. "So you told him that you'd have to find her and ask?"

Lisa smiled her prettiest fake smile. "Mike, who struck you out last time we played baseball?"

Mike gulped and turned red. "Um, you, the, uh, most beautiful girl in the world."

"Come on, guys," I said. "We've only got a few days left here."

Mike snorted. "So that's why you got Ralphy to ask J. P. about mail, Lisa to call her uncle in Washington, and me to find a bucket."

Put in those terms, it did sound stupid. But I wasn't yet ready to tell them what I had learned from State Trooper Boyd, not unless everything else fit together first. Ralphy's information had not helped.

I leaned forward to explain.

The couches here were set in an informal square. To my left, the fireplace crackled and hissed. Ahead, and across the small coffee table that propped my cast, were Ralphy, Mike, and Lisa. Beneath the table was the plastic bucket Mike had borrowed from a laundry room. On all of my friends' faces were strange smiles.

"Come on, Mike," I started to say. "I'm not that crazy—"

I didn't finish, because a lasso settled over me. Which, at least, explained the strange smiles. They'd seen Joel's approach behind me.

"Thanks for the warning, guys." I yanked the thin nylon rope and reeled Joel in like a fish.

"Hey, pard," I told him, "You've made me a steer one too many times. This rope is going with your gun caps."

I unlassoed myself, grabbed my ski jacket from beside me on the couch, rolled the rope into a small, flat bundle, and stuffed it into the large inner pocket of my ski jacket. That left Joel with his cowboy hat, cowboy boots, and an empty revolver. He was gone with all three before I'd finished putting the rope away.

"Ricky," Lisa said, "with what my uncle told me, I think I can see a reason for your questions."

"We might have a motive?" I felt excitement edge back into my stomach.

She nodded. "But I'm not sure I like the direction it leads—"

"Hey, guys," Mike pleaded. "You're making about as much sense as Ralphy when he starts talking computer language."

"Motive," Ralphy explained. "That's the reason behind the action taken or directed by a person or organization—"

"Where's the bucket?" Mike growled. "We can put it over Ralphy's head. Of course I know what motive means. But why are you guys talking about it?"

"The accidents around here don't make sense unless we can figure out who has something to gain from them," I said. "If we can figure out why, that might point to who."

"And," Lisa added, "my uncle was able to confirm a powerful *Why*. It's just that I don't like the *Who* it points toward."

Mike slapped his head with both his hands. "I give up."

"Don't," I said. "Just ask yourself who gains the most as the value of the Zebulon resort drops."

He thought for a moment. "That's easy. The group of Japanese investors who are trying to buy it. This afternoon you explained why Abe Avery didn't want to bring the police in to investigate—because it would lower the price, and Abe promised it wasn't cheating because the value would equal the price as soon as the accidents stopped."

It was my turn to nod. "Say the resort was worth ten million bucks. Business drops, it gets a bad name, and now it's only worth two million."

Ralphy spoke. "Just like a comic book story. You know, where someone rigs up fake ghosts so that everyone thinks the house is haunted, then buys the house real cheap."

"You bet!" Mike snapped his fingers. "And those businessmen must be real mad you found the gasoline time bomb. They were probably expecting another couple hundred thousand to be dropped from the price by the time they arrived here today."

I stopped him from speaking more. "I thought that, too, but there's a big problem with blaming the Japanese businessmen."

"Access," Lisa guessed. "How could they arrange for all the accidents to happen?"

I shook my head. "Nope. Put yourself in their shoes. To save eight million dollars, don't you think it'd be easy to hire somebody here on the inside to do the dirty work?"

"Time," Ralphy said. "This afternoon you told us the accidents started about a year ago. But you also told us the Japanese didn't start looking to buy until August, barely four months ago."

I shook my head again. "Nope. Still put yourself in their shoes. Say you decided a year and a half ago you might want to make an offer. Wouldn't you start the accidents as soon as possible, then wait as long as possible until you showed interest in buying?"

Ralphy shrugged agreement.

"The ghost!" Mike said. "How do you explain the gold miner's daughter?"

"Exactly," I said.

"But no matter who you decide gains from dropping the value," Ralphy argued, "there's still the problem of the ghost."

"Maybe," I said. "Maybe not. Let's hear what Lisa's uncle said."

"He cautioned me first that he's not an inheritance tax expert," Lisa began.

Ralphy's and Mike's eyes grew wide.

"Yup," I said as they understood the implications. "Doesn't it all tie together? Abe finds out he's going to die, Robert moves here, and accidents begin to happen. All about a year ago."

Lisa nodded. "My uncle said that tax laws are not always the same from state to state. But he said that in general, a huge part of any estate goes to the government in the form of taxes."

I took a deep breath. "And did he say anything about how they might value something as complicated as a ski resort?"

Lisa looked me directly in the eyes. "He agreed that a legitimate offer to purchase could be argued as fair market value."

"No way," Mike said. "No way, no way, no way."

"Triplicate for me," Ralphy said. "No way."

"Who else is an insider?" I asked. "Who else has been here about a year, about as long as the accidents have been happening? Who else stands to gain if Zebulon drops in value? Who else is able to end the accidents and build Zebulon up again after Abe Avery has left him the ski resort?"

Mike stood and paced tight circles. "Are you saying Robert Avery is trying to get out of paying inheritance taxes? That an offer to purchase this place at way less than what it is worth will be taken as its true value by government tax people?"

"Do your math: It's worth ten million and has an offer for two million," I said. "Thirty percent tax on ten million is three million dollars. Thirty percent tax on two million is only six hundred thousand dollars. He saves himself a cool two point four million."

"I don't believe it," Mike said.

"The only trouble is, my letter theory doesn't hold up."

"Huh?"

I explained what I'd decided after discovering that Abe Avery didn't have a typewriter and finished with my conclusion. "If Robert Avery was starting all this trouble, it would make sense that he didn't want Miss Avery to discover it. So instead of censoring the letters, he would just replace them. Since he couldn't imitate Abe's handwriting, he'd switch to a typewriter."

I took another breath. "But Ralphy's answer blew that theory to shreds. J. P. takes the mail, not Robert."

Now Ralphy's eyes were so wide I could see the fire flickering off them in reflection.

"You didn't let me finish," he said. "Because J. P. told me that his father then takes all the family mail from him and insists on driving it into the nearest town."

We all became silent as we thought about what this could mean. Ralphy, Mike, and Lisa were probably with me in this. We didn't want to believe that Robert was behind it.

"It's back to the ghost," Mike finally said. "This theory fits everything, except for the ghost."

"Unfortunately not," I said.

They all stared at me.

"Mike, fill this bucket with firewood, then carry it across the room and leave it there."

He blinked at my unexpected request but after a few moments did so.

"Lisa, could you go pick it up and carry it back?"

She gave me a puzzled look but brought it back to me.

"And Ralphy," I said, "could you carry it around the couches?"

He did, then sat.

"So," Mike said, "What does that prove?"

"I think a lot. How did each of you carry it?"

"With our hands?"

I rolled my eyeballs. "Let me put it this way, Mike. Grab the bucket handle but with your palm down, so that the top of your wrist faces the ceiling."

"You mean overhanded, because we all carried it—"

"—underhanded," I finished for him.

He tried lifting it that way. "Doesn't feel right. I can lift better with my hand below the handle, palm upward."

"All three of you did it that way. The natural way."

"But what does that prove?"

"Think of the ghost," I replied. "How was she carrying the lantern?"

A brief pause, then all three spoke at once. "Overhanded!"

I nodded. It was time to tell them about the results of my call to State Trooper Boyd.

CHAPTER 21

All the next day, while the others went skiing so that things seemed normal, I followed Robert Avery as much as possible.

We only had suspicions at this point—the who and the why. To *prove* both, though, we needed the how. I was hoping for something, anything, to suggest that proof.

The task itself was not difficult. Robert was a tall man. He wore a distinctive purple ski jacket and, of course, had no reason to hide his movements as he strode from one part of Zebulon to another.

On the other hand, I was nearly invisible as a smaller figure among all the skiers and resort guests who moved throughout Zebulon. I always had my ski goggles on my forehead, ready to be dropped across my face should Robert ever turn around. And I was supposed to be in the leg cast that I'd left behind in my room. Who would suspect me as a pursuer?

Trouble was, easy as the following became, not much happened.

Robert spent most of the morning in his office at the main resort building. Which meant I spent most of the morning in the entranceway of the next nearest building, stamping my feet to stay warm as I watched the entrance of his building.

He spent lunch at the café in the lodge near the chair lift. My only consolation was that I could eat in the opposite corner as I watched him. I didn't dare, however, remove my ski jacket, and I had to keep my ski hat low over my face, so I nearly sweated to death.

In the afternoon he went back to the office and stayed there. I froze again in my outdoor surveillance position.

The next morning was the same. He went nowhere unusual, met no one unusual, did nothing that would suggest any proof of how the accidents had happened. It was so boring, I even started to doubt that he was behind it all.

The next afternoon was also the same.

But the day after became the killer.

"Two days left," Mike said over breakfast at the main resort building, "with nothing to show for your Sherlock Holmes act. I'm beginning to believe that all the accidents were bad luck and that—"

"Wipe the chocolate milk off your face," I grumbled.

"—the fact that we were sent here is great luck," he continued without losing a beat.

"Yeah, yeah, yeah," I said.

"You don't mind missing all this time on the slopes with your fake broken leg? We're getting to be good skiers, you know."

"Yeah, yeah, yeah," I said. Two days of boring surveillance work will do that to a person—rob him of enthusiasm—especially when I didn't want to admit that I did feel dumb for missing all that time on the slopes.

Mike shrugged. "Well, time to go. Daylight's wasting, and Ralphy and Lisa and Joel are nearly out the door."

"Mike," I pointed out, "they've been waiting there for the last five minutes while you finished your third helping of pancakes."

"Details." He dismissed my observation with a wave of his hand as he threw on his ski jacket. With a wink, he spun on his heels and ran to catch up to the others. Lisa gave me a wave from the doorway, as did Ralphy. Joel just pulled his cowboy hat lower on his head before following them out.

That left me alone with the bottom half of a cup of hot chocolate. I finished it slowly. Like someone who had been fishing in the same spot for days with no results, I saw little reason to hurry back to the stupid doorway for the wonderful privilege of watching for Robert Avery's predictable entrances and exits from his office.

A few minutes later, then, as other skiers wandered in and out of the cafeteria, I grabbed my crutches and started to hobble back to the hotel room, where I would discard the cast.

I had just stepped outside when I noticed Robert Avery's tall figure and purple jacket across the parking lot.

For a moment I froze, then remembered that until I was out of the cast and officially following him, I had nothing to hide.

It wouldn't have mattered anyway. Robert Avery did not notice me. He walked a straight, purposeful line toward the back corner of the next nearest resort building.

I made a brilliant deduction. He was going somewhere, and the somewhere was not his office.

Now I had to make a brilliant decision. Go back to the hotel room, lose my cast, and risk losing him? Or stay on crutches, stay with him, but risk getting caught?

Then I realized that if I stayed on crutches and acted as if I had nothing to hide, my actions would seem innocent anyway. I would just be a dumb kid coming over to say hello.

I stumped in his direction as quickly as possible.

He reached the back corner of the building long before I did and, instead of going inside through the rear entrance, marched behind and out of sight.

A few minutes later when I arrived at the back of the building, I paused, then stuck my head around the corner to see what he was doing.

I saw only snow, trees, and a wooden shed, weathered almost black.

Beyond that shed a series of trails led up the side of the mountain. But there was no sign of Robert Avery.

Had he gone beyond the shed and up the mountain? If so, I would have to hurry back to my room and get rid of my awkward cast before attempting the hike.

Only one way to find out. I hobbled the seventy-five feet to the side of the shed. I already had a question prepared if he found me. I'd ask him if there was anything I could help him with, because I'd seen him walk this way and I was getting bored doing nothing in my cast.

There were no sounds from inside the shed.

But no footprints going up the hill.

I went to the front of the shed, where an ancient padlock secured the door shut.

How could Robert Avery be inside? The shed was padlocked on the outside. Nobody shuts a door, then from the inside of a building reaches through the door and locks it on the outside.

Why was an old shed tucked away in the trees at such a modern resort? I studied the front of the shed more carefully. Weather and time had slowly worked the slats apart. The cracks were wide enough that I could peek inside. Stripes of sunlight fell onto the uneven floor inside, and I could clearly identify the shapes of large iron machinery. I could also see that Robert Avery was not inside.

But no footprints led away from this packed path into the un-touched snow on the trails past the shed.

I stepped back to confirm there were no footprints anywhere else, and I noticed that a dusting of snow covered a small plaque above the door. It took only one swipe with an outstretched glove to clear the snow away.

Zebulon Gold, Incorporated 1879.

Part of the old gold mine?

The padlock looked old enough to fit the part. Except—

I leaned closer.

Except shiny scratches covered the base of the bolt where it entered the padlock. The lock had been opened recently.

I pulled, and it popped loose.

Now I was really confused. This meant Robert Avery, too, could go inside. But I was still faced with the question of how he could have closed the padlock on the outside from his position on the inside. And if he had gone inside, how had he disappeared? There was no sign of him in there.

On the other hand, no footsteps led away. So unless he had simply flown upward . . .

I'd like to blame frustration and boredom and stupidity. It had been a few days of doing nothing. We seemed so close, yet we were so far away from any solutions. And someone, after all, had nearly gotten me killed by cutting the rope on the ski patrol toboggan.

But it was curiosity that got me to open the door and step inside, curiosity I was sure that I could explain to Robert Avery if he was actually in there, too.

I shut the door behind me.

Nothing happened. No shouts. No accusations. No bad guys beaning me over the head.

My eyes adjusted to the sunlight that filtered through the cracks.

As I had first guessed, there was just heavy equipment. Pumps and pulleys. Large metal-spoked, metal-rimmed wheels. Huge cylinders. All rusted and mute.

I balanced on my crutches and tried to make sense of the equipment.

Two of the pulleys here were lined up and down, just like the giant pulleys were lined horizontally at the bottom of the chair lifts.

Hey!

The chair-lift pulleys moved the thick cable that pulled the ski chairs up the hill. Would these pulleys move a cable up and down directly below them?

And if the answer was yes, maybe this shed was built above a main shaft of the gold mine.

I inched closer to see.

The outlines of a huge trapdoor showed on the floor beneath those old, rusted pulleys.

Then, of course, my heart wanted to stop beating.

Trapdoor?

As in where Robert Avery could have gone?

As in where Robert Avery might appear from any second?

I made a real quick decision.

Get out now. Return later and find out what was hidden there.

I backed away from the trapdoor, half expecting it to rise any second.

Then I relaxed again.

You knothead, I told myself, *how can Robert Avery be in here with the padlock shut on the outside?*

At the door I saw something I didn't want to see.

A loose board.

I pushed. It moved outward.

Rats.

Someone could easily reach outside from in here and from the inside move that outside padlock back into position.

My heart wanted again to stop beating. Because this meant Robert Avery truly was inside, right beneath the trapdoor.

How close had I come to getting caught?

I didn't want to guess, just wanted to leave.

I stepped outside into the bright sunlight.

For a moment I was blinded after the time in the dimness of the shed. But I wasn't too blinded to see a blurring movement at the side of my head.

It was all I saw.

The sunlight ended as my world caved in on me in a crushing suddenness of black pain.

CHAPTER 22

I didn't want to open my eyes. Not when my head felt the size of a watermelon.

"Why does the kid have to die?"

Now I really didn't want to open my eyes. Groggy as I was, I recognized Robert Avery's voice. It didn't take a rocket surgeon to decide he was talking about me.

"I'll give you twelve or thirteen million reasons," a voice answered. *Thelma?* "And each of those reasons is green and has a picture of George Washington."

I squinted my eyes open, just a crack.

It *was* Thelma!

"No money is worth killing someone," Robert told her.

I wanted to cheer.

"Then try this reason," Thelma replied, ice in her voice. "You've gone so far already, it's too late to turn around."

There was a silence.

I tried to figure out where I was, but without opening my eyes completely so that they'd guess I was awake, it was difficult. I was lying on hard-packed dirt. All I could see was a huge table above me and to the right. Some extension cords across the ground. And the legs and feet of Thelma and Robert as they paced away from me.

"Too late to turn around?" Robert Avery said, almost in disbelief. "Is that a threat?"

"Partners don't threaten partners, darling." Thelma's voice went from its previous ice to soothing warmth. "Not a threat at all. It's merely a statement of fact. This snoopy kid is a problem. If you don't get rid of the problem, we lose everything. And go to jail."

Robert Avery's legs stopped pacing.

"I ... just ... don't know," he said. "It was never supposed to get this complicated—"

Thelma's legs moved close to his. I guessed by the tone of her voice she was giving him a hug. "It will be over soon."

My throat was now dry with fear. Easy for her to say. No one was talking about *her* death.

Then I thought of a way out. If I could convince them that I knew nothing—

First I groaned, as if just starting to wake. Then I rolled, as if struggling to my feet. I discovered that it really was a struggle to get to my feet. It did not make me feel better to know I could blame it on getting knocked out twice in one week.

I managed to sit.

Thelma and Robert looked down on me.

"Hi," I croaked. "I can't believe it."

They frowned.

"Falling on my crutches," I explained. "I know I shouldn't have been, but I was snooping in an old shed because I guessed it was part of the gold mine. Then I think I fell on my way out—"

Still they said nothing.

"Whoever brought me here probably already explained, huh. I'm sorry for the trouble, but I didn't see any 'no trespassing' signs on the shed—"

Robert extended a hand to help me to my feet.

"My head," I said. "It hurts, but I think I'm okay. I guess both of you got called here for no reason."

I looked around. "Where is here? It doesn't look like a first-aid office."

Now that I was standing, I could see more. The room was the size of a small garage. Narrow iron pipes crisscrossed the rock ceiling. A couple of bright, bare bulbs hung from wooden crossbeams. The huge table held video equipment. There were mirrors set up in random places. A long, narrow black box with an extending tube was on a tripod, aimed at one of the mirrors. Two computers sat on a desk in the opposite corner. And beneath the desk was some crumpled clothing, topped by what appeared to be a wig.

"Don't play dumb." Thelma's snarl brought me back from my study of the room, and her eyes bored directly into mine. It was like looking into the flat green eyes of a snake. "I saw you following Robert."

So much for my plan of innocent ignorance.

"I wanted to ask—"

"And that's why you were snooping around the inside of the shed?"

This woman was scary. She could go from sweet and nice to poisonous and mean. I remembered how she had seemed so caring and concerned as she poured tea for Abe Avery. Now...

I shivered.

"Aw, Thelma," Robert said, "the kid was probably just bored, sitting around all day with that broken leg. He probably wasn't up to anything."

"Doesn't matter, does it? It doesn't matter why he made a decision to follow you inside. I made a decision to play it safe and knock him out as he was leaving," she replied without taking her eyes from mine. "He's here now and has seen too much."

The finality of her voice made me shiver again. I had no doubt that she wouldn't let me out of here alive.

Another thought blasted into my head. Maybe the opposite of innocence would work. I'd seen enough movies where people had left sealed information with their lawyers—a kind of reverse blackmail that saved their lives.

So I took a breath and hit them with my best shot.

"This is where you make holograms of the ghost, isn't it? Three-dimensional images of light that appear real but don't cast shadows or leave footprints."

Thelma sucked in her breath. It was enough of an answer for me to plunge ahead.

"We're somewhere in the old gold mine, aren't we? The perfect workshop. Hidden, unknown. Thelma puts on the dress and wig in the corner there and does the acting while Robert films to make the hologram."

"How—" Robert tried to break in.

I didn't let him. "The ghost we saw from your father's place moved ten steps and then looked back. Moved ten steps, then looked back. Kept repeating the same movement. This room is about ten steps long."

"But—"

"So you shot the hologram here and duplicated it. I presume these computers are part of it. And the black box with the tube generates a laser, split by the mirrors."

Robert's wide eyes confirmed everything that I'd suspected when that sudden beam of sunlight had reminded me about Ralphy's lecture on how to make a hologram postcard and how concentrated light did such amazing things.

"But you shouldn't have had Thelma carry the lantern," I said. "Most people carry things underhanded. Not Thelma. She pours tea the same way she carries a lantern. Overhanded. With her left hand. An old skiing accident, I believe. Her wrist has never been the same. The ghost carried the lantern in her left hand. It was too much of a coincidence."

Both their mouths gaped. Whatever advantage I had, I needed to push now, no matter how badly my head ached.

"Of course," I continued, "it wasn't until my friend Ralphy had heard that Robert was a laser expert for the military that we were able to put it together."

"We?" Robert echoed weakly.

"We," I said firmly. I was arguing for my life. I couldn't show any fear. "And I had someone make a phone call to find out exactly what you did for the military."

"That's not public information!"

I thought of State Trooper Boyd's groan when I had asked him to find out. How he had had to call a friend higher up for a favor, who had had to call a friend in Washington, D.C., who had had to call a CIA friend, and so on until a half dozen favors had been called in by a half dozen people and the information relayed all the way back down.

"A laser specialist in holograms. You were working on a way to replicate soldiers in 3-D. What was the theory?" I listened in my mind to Trooper Boyd's explanation. "Oh yes. If the enemy can't tell which one is a real soldier approaching and which one is merely a light image of a soldier, how will the enemy know where to concentrate its firepower? And what better way to make fifty soldiers seem like an army of a thousand? Especially if you can come up with the portable equipment to generate those images anywhere you want. Like on a mountainside—"

Robert began to sputter. "Thelma, this is much worse than—"

"Shut up," she said quietly. "Let the kid talk."

I tried to hammer them with everything I had. "Hologram ghosts and tax inheritance fraud—"

Robert looked for a place to sit and bowed his head.

I told them everything that had pointed us toward figuring it out. When I finished five minutes later, the room was so silent, I could hear the dripping of water condensation from old pipes.

"Why tell us this?" Thelma finally asked.

"So you know that we know."

"There's that 'we' again," she said. "Who is 'we'?"

It was time to play my main card, to hit them with my best bluff. I had to convince them that they would be caught, even if I were silenced. Then they'd have no reason to silence me; adding murder to their crimes would only make things worse for them.

"The 'we' are all my friends here," I said. "They know everything. If I'm not back by the time they finish skiing, they're going to the police."

More drops of water plinked onto the floor in the eerie quiet as we stared at each other.

Then Thelma laughed so softly that again shivers played up and down my spine.

"Two things wrong with your bluff, kid," she said.

I waited.

"One, they can't know about the gold mine shaft and this room. And without this mine chamber, all they have are guesses. Otherwise, you'd have gone to the police earlier."

My throat tightened. This woman had glacier water for blood.

"And two—"

Her words caressed me, as if she were a cat playing with a mouse.

"—when your friends die in a chair-lift accident this afternoon, all that information will go with them, won't it, now?"

CHAPTER 23

Thelma told Robert to lay me on my back and tie each of my hands to opposite legs of the table.

"Come on, Thelma. We can bolt the door on the outside. He'll never escape, and even if he did, how's he going to climb the shafts with a broken leg in a cast?"

Thelma rolled her eyes in impatience. "What's to stop him from wrecking our equipment?"

"My word of honor?" I tried.

Thelma snorted. "Right."

"We can't leave him on the ground," Robert said. "As soon as we pull the power, it'll get cold. No need to torture the kid."

"So stand him up if you're so determined to bleed for the kid. Tie his hands above his head and loop the cord over the pipes. In the long run he won't care anyway."

Robert shrugged apologetically in my direction. "Don't struggle," he said. "You'll only get knocked over the head again."

I held my hands out. He wrapped them quickly and efficiently with a length of cord, threw the other end over the pipe, pulled it toward him to raise my hands, and then tied the free end around my wrist.

He leaned toward me as he tied, close enough that I could smell aftershave and count the individual stubbles of bristle on his chin.

He murmured words into my ear without taking his eyes off the knot tying.

"I can't murder," he said, "not for any money. I've left you enough slack to walk and stay warm. I'll be back in half an hour."

Did I hear right?

I didn't dare ask. Not with Thelma nearby.

I could only hope and pray as the lights went out.

At the count of 7,321, I gave up hope. My arms ached from holding them above me, my head hurt, and I was scared.

By my calculations, much more than two hours had passed. I had waited in the darkness—and it was so black here in the depths of the earth that I couldn't tell the difference between eyes open and eyes closed.

I'd spent the first while talking out loud to myself, telling myself what an idiot I was for the bluff that meant my friends would have died in a chair-lift accident if Robert Avery hadn't decided against murder.

Then I had shut up, because I was sure a half hour had passed, and I tried not to think that my friends might really die because I'd been an idiot.

Then I told myself that no, time passes really slowly when you're in a private burial chamber with nothing but the dripping of water to keep you company.

Then the water stopped dripping and I missed the noise. Then I realized why the water had stopped dripping. It was getting cold. Then I decided that meant maybe close to half an hour had passed, so to be sure, I started counting as I paced and hobbled back and forth— like a dog on a leash—to keep warm.

Sixty meant a minute. Thirty-six hundred meant an hour. At 7,321 I couldn't fool myself any longer.

I finally faced what I didn't want to face.

Robert Avery was probably not coming back. Maybe he'd said so just to give me hope or to delay my efforts at escape. Even if he was returning, how much longer could I wait? Well over two hours had passed—I could assume it was already early afternoon. I didn't know what time they intended to cause the chair-lift accident to happen.

Each of my heartbeats was one heartbeat closer to the promised deaths of my friends. Even if I could get loose from this rope, the massive door to this chamber was bolted shut on the outside. And outside that door, what kind of maze of mineshafts waited for me to find my way to the surface?

I'll never admit that I cried. But I can say that when salt water freezes in tiny drops on a guy's face, it hurts. It drove me nuts not to be able to reach with my hands and rub. Not only did my face itch, but my leg within the cast within my ski pants—

Cast!

I groaned at my stupidity. I'd been so concerned about Robert's return, I hadn't given any thought to helping myself.

But what could I do to get rid of the cast? And what next from there?

Whoa, I told myself, *worry about one thing at a time.*

I sagged against the rope to rest my arms and thought of the cast.

The pipe above me crossed the length of the room. With the rope looped over that pipe I could travel back and forth the length but go no farther than a half step away from the pipe.

Even if I could reach something to scrape off the bands that held the two halves of the cast together, I'd still have to get my ski pants off.

What if . . .

Okay, maybe . . .

I kicked off my one boot, then the larger one that Abe Avery had found to put over the casted foot.

I pressed the heel of my cast over the edge of the bottom of the pants on my other leg. Then pulled my other leg upward.

The waistline of my ski pants dropped a quarter inch.

I switched feet. Placed my socked toes on the fringe of the pants along my cast and lifted the casted leg. My pants waistline dropped fractionally again.

Then I pressed my cast-heel on the other side and repeated the process. Went back to using my sock foot on the other side. Repeated the process again and again until finally my ski pants dropped to my knees. I was able to shake the pants loose from my good leg, stand on the loose pants of the other leg, and slowly pull my cast free.

Hah!

It was a short-lived feeling of triumph.

I was standing in sock feet and long underwear, a cast on one leg, my hands above my head, my boots scattered somewhere in the freezing cold darkness, and very able to understand what it meant when someone says he doesn't know whether to laugh or cry.

Now what? I told myself it would be faster to die from exposure to the cold than from starvation, so I worked the sock loose from my good foot.

My toes were nearly numb already.

I leaned on my casted leg and lifted my good leg. With my toes, I felt for the lower band on my cast. Once it was wedged between my big toe and the next one, I started to wriggle it downward.

I was an ice block when the band finally slid off the casted foot. But an ice block with two cast halves attached only by an upper rubber band. My leg was able to wiggle freely between the halves, but I knew there was no way I could lift my foot high enough to reach the second band.

I started hopping and shaking.

That served two purposes. It warmed me up again, and little by little, the flopping cast halves were slipping loose of the last band.

Then, with a gentle thud that seemed loud in the tomb-like silence, the cast fell free, and the upper rubber band slid down my leg.

What next?

I moved along the pipe until I got to the far wall. I grabbed the rope with my hands, leaned back against the rope, and used that leverage to walk up the wall. My feet didn't reach the pipe above me until I was almost upside down and my shoulders were strained to the breaking point from holding against the rope.

I hooked my legs over the pipe and, with a lot of grunting, pulled myself up the rope until my hands were able to grab the pipe.

I was completely upside down now. Ski jacket on my upper half. Long underwear on my bottom half. Legs wrapped around the pipe. Hands on the pipe directly above my face. And most important, by bending my face forward, able to bury my nose in my wrists.

That meant my teeth could reach the first knot that kept the rope attached over the pipe.

I gnawed at the rope—a desperate, cold puppy chewing at bone. Then an end of the rope worked loose from the knot. Another loop worked loose. And another.

My hands were free of the pipe.

I lowered my feet and dropped.

The fall nearly killed me. In the darkness, I had no idea when to expect ground. And my feet were so frozen, it felt like I broke every bone in my heels.

It didn't matter.

When I rolled over and onto my feet, I was standing straight and could lower my arms. The second knot, the one that held my hands together, took me another five minutes of frantic biting and chewing.

When the rope hit my feet, I could hardly believe it.

I clenched and unclenched my fists, groaning in pain as the blood eased back into my hands to give me a world record dose of pins and needles. Then I crawled around in the darkness to feel around for my ski pants and boots.

I was one warm, grateful puppy when I finally got all my clothes back on.

Unfortunately, between me and freedom remained the bolted door and the mine shafts.

But, thanks to my pesky brother, Joel, and the tiny air vent above me that would suck smoke clear, I had a plan for that, too.

CHAPTER 24

Safety experts would recommend that you refrain from grabbing a truck's rear bumper while it is in motion. But safety experts rarely need to worry that their friends might die on a chair lift at any time.

So as the truck slowed for a corner, I jumped out from behind a tree, ducked low to remain hidden from the rearview mirror, grabbed the bumper, and crouched.

On the snowy road, my feet worked as skis as the truck picked up speed. This seemed the fastest way to the top of the road that led to Abe's house.

I'd thought this final part through during my scramble in the last mine shaft.

It was already two o'clock, and I had no idea when the chair-lift accident would happen. I didn't dare risk a waste of time to search the vast slopes for my friends. Nor did I dare risk a waste of time trying to convince various resort employees that my friends were in danger. Who would believe some twelve-year-old kid enough to shut down an entire ski hill?

No, there was only one person with enough authority to make the single phone call that would cut the power to all the chair lifts—Abe Avery.

Which was why I now clung to the rear bumper of a truck and watched the blur of snow whiz beneath my feet. It was like water skiing, except no rope, no skis, and no water to cushion my fall should I lose balance. I spun side to side as my boots bounced off various stones buried in the snow, but there was no way that I would let go. Not at this speed. Not with a chair-lift accident waiting to kill my friends.

The truck finally slowed, then stopped.

I was up on my feet and running around the side of the truck even before the driver got his door open.

"Hey!" he shouted.

I ignored him, took the steps to Abe's cabin in one jump, and pounded on the door.

Seconds later the door opened to show another Zebulon employee, dressed in the same green jacket as the driver trying to catch up behind me.

"Abe here?" I gasped.

"Yes, but—"

I pushed past him and dashed through the hallway.

"Abe! Abe!" I shouted.

My momentum carried me to the living room. "Abe! Abe!"

I expected protests. I expected that I'd have to make a convincing argument to get him to believe me. I even expected that Abe would be crushed to hear that his own son had planned the accidents.

I didn't expect to see Thelma in the living room.

Abe stood at the living room window, staring out over the valley. Thelma stood close beside him, a hand on his shoulder.

They both turned at my shouts.

"Abe, you, um—" I couldn't get any more words out. My mind was numb to see Thelma here.

The two resort employees reached the room. "Boss, we tried to stop the kid."

"It's okay," Abe said. He waved them away.

"Hello, Ricky," Thelma said in a quiet voice as the men backed out. "As you might guess, this is not the best of times to visit."

Abe turned back to the window. My brief glimpse of his face showed that he was in tremendous pain.

"Wh-wh-what?" I couldn't have been more stunned if she had slammed me across the head with a baseball bat. Wasn't this the woman who had passed a death sentence on me only hours earlier?

"I'm not trying to be rude," she said quickly, "but Abe's very upset right now, and as his nurse, I've asked that no visitors be allowed."

"B-but y-you, you—" I wanted to tell her that she was the one who had actually stopped to smile hatred at me as she shut the door to bury me alive in the depths of a mine.

"You seem upset, too," she soothed. "Did one of the men at the door tell you?"

My mouth opened and closed a few times as I tried to speak.

How could she be such a good actor? Or had I somehow imagined the entire morning?

"It's about Robert," she said. "You remember? Abe's son. He's been badly hurt."

Abe finally left the window. "I'll tell him," he said, his voice heavy with grief. "It was an explosion. In one of the storage rooms. He's now in a coma."

And I was now going to tell this deeply saddened man that Robert had been trying to destroy the resort? Yet my friends were in danger.

"The power—" I began. I needed to get those chair-lifts shut down.

"No power on the ski hill," Abe said. "It was a storage room near the main generator."

"Oh."

"That's not the worst of it," Thelma said in gentle tones. "It looks like Robert was behind all the accidents at the ski hill."

"Oh." There's not much else to say when it feels like a heavyweight boxer is rocking you with head punches. She hadn't even shown surprise to see me. A normal person would have gone into shock at the appearance of someone left for dead.

"We're all upset by it," she continued. "They found timers, dynamite, everything in that room. It seems like that has been his base all along."

Abe shuffled to the couch and sat down. He buried his head in his hands. "The worst part," he said, his voice muffled, "is that I've suspected him for months. I could have stopped this earlier. And he wouldn't now be in a hospital room, attached to a life-support machine."

In a flash, I understood. Abe hadn't kept the authorities away from the previous accident scenes because he wanted the Japanese to make a good offer. He was afraid they might find out who had been responsible. And he loved his son so much that now he was in deep grief not because of the accidents but because Robert's life might end.

I understood something else. The reason Robert hadn't returned to save me from my burial chamber. And that reason was standing in front of me.

"Sir," I said to Abe, "I think your son was on the verge of telling you everything."

Abe looked up sharply. "How can you say that?"

I pointed at Thelma. "But she stopped him."

Thelma blinked. "I don't understand, Ricky."

Even now, her response was such that I hardly believed myself. If I didn't push on now, I might not ever.

"Your son caused some accidents," I said. "But none that would seriously hurt people. He was even careful enough to start an avalanche when he knew that the run would be closed for the day. And when it came down to murder, he couldn't do it."

"Murder?" Abe echoed.

"Mine," I said firmly. "And my friends."

Thelma sat beside Abe and pressed one of his large, gnarled hands between hers. "Abe," she said softly, "it will be all right."

She looked at me and her voice rose in anger. "It's hardly appropriate to play such a cruel joke on this man. I think you should leave now."

I gritted my teeth and shook my head. I plunged into the explanation of all that had happened this morning.

When I finished, Abe searched Thelma's eyes. "The boy can't be lying, can he?"

Thelma's eyes were wide. "I suppose we can easily see if there is a mine chamber like the one he described. But I don't understand why he's trying to involve me."

Thelma stood and almost pleaded, "Why, Ricky? I haven't done anything to hurt you."

"I can't believe this," I said. "You told Robert to shut me in there. He didn't want to."

"Abe, I'm sorry," she said. "I think it's because he's trying to make you feel better about your son."

She paused, then pointed at my leg. "Why, Abe, notice he's no longer in a cast. He's been lying to all of us about a broken leg. This is just another lie."

I felt myself redden. "I can explain it, really." My confusion and embarrassment made my voice so shaky, I barely believed me.

Abe closed his eyes. "I don't know what to believe. Ricky, do you have proof?"

"About Thelma?"

Abe nodded.

"I ... I ..." My mouth kept working as my thoughts scrambled to arrange themselves in any kind of order. No, I couldn't prove it. It would be her word against mine. "I ... I ... have—"

Okay, I thought, try one last bluff.

"I have a state trooper named John Boyd," I said.

For a moment Thelma's face lost its innocence, and she darted a look of hatred at me. Her features immediately became soft again.

Ho, ho. A tiny crack. But how can I widen it?

"Yes." I spoke slowly, trying to guess what was the weak point. "When I called him earlier to discover what your son did for the military, I also called him to check out one other suspect. Thelma."

She resumed patting Abe's hand.

Why wasn't she worried now? I'd just told her that she had been checked out. But she felt safe. Unless it was because I'd used the word *Thelma* . . .

If she was this evil—I couldn't think of a better word to describe someone who could act so innocent after leaving one person in a burial chamber and arranging for a dynamite accident to take care of another—would this be her first crime? And if it wasn't her first crime, wouldn't she cover herself by changing her name?

I tried that stab in the dark.

"But I didn't ask State Trooper Boyd to check her out by name. I gave him her license plate number."

"What!" she screeched. Sudden rage rearranged her face into an ugly mask.

Bingo. How well could I continue the bluff? But she was off balance, and I was able to hide my triumph with a shrug. "How else could I find out who you really were—"

She rose, screaming, "You meddling twerp. I'll rip your eyeballs from your head." She jumped at me. I put up my hands to fend her off. Nothing happened.

She leaped past me and down the hallway.

I turned to give chase.

It was too late. By the time I got to the door, she had reached the truck parked and idling out front, gunning it away from the startled driver, who stood in the snow and watched her disappear.

Epilogue

"Psychopath," I told Miss Avery. "Thelma is a psychopath. Someone with no conscience. Capable of inflicting tremendous evil without caring how much it hurts anyone. That's how State Trooper Boyd explained it to me."

Here in the quiet solitude of the visitors' room of the old folks' home in Jamesville, hundreds of miles away from Zebulon, I still shivered to think of Thelma. One of her smiles made you feel like the most special person in the world, and another could make you feel as if you were a fly and she were pulling your wings loose.

Miss Avery leaned forward in her chair. She pulled her shawl over her shoulders. "Yes," she said, "Abe told me that she was a skilled actress. Enough to fool Robert."

Now *that* was a complicated subject. Love. Fortunately, I understood enough of it to know I understood nothing of it.

Instead, I explained to Miss Avery what I did know about the rest.

Robert, out of his coma by that night, had said that, in love and believing he was loved in turn, he rigged a few minor accidents at her urging. By the time he saw how much pain it was causing Abe, he wanted to quit, but she blackmailed him into continuing by sweetly pointing out he was already in enough trouble so he might as well continue. Besides, she had argued, wouldn't Abe want him to have as big an inheritance as possible, even if it took some tax fraud? And who could get hurt by that?

When it came to murder, though, Robert decided the price was too high. After leaving me in the mine chamber, he had told Thelma that he was through. He was returning to get me. He'd tell Abe everything before letting innocent people die.

At that point Thelma had pulled a gun from her purse, moved him to the storage room, and told him to turn around. He did. She knocked him across the back of the head and set the dynamite to blow, knowing that even if Mike and Lisa and Ralphy did have a way of proving something, the blame would fall on Robert. The only thing that went wrong was that Robert survived the explosion.

The police in Colorado suspected that as a private nurse, Thelma had the perfect excuse to return to the hospital later to find a way to end Robert's life while he lay in a coma. He, of course, was the only link to prove that she was not Thelma Gibbons but rather a federally wanted criminal by the name of Carol Madimsky.

"State Trooper Boyd has also spoken to me," Miss Avery said as I finished that part. "They tracked down her real identity through her fingerprints. Abe wasn't the first rich and dying man that she has tried to scam."

I knew that, too. Apparently, as a nurse, she watched for the perfect victim. An older man, wealthy, and not so close to dying that she wouldn't have time to gain his confidence and find a way to take part of his fortune. Then she'd clear town, work as a private nurse in a different state under a different name, and like a spider on a web, patiently wait to find another.

In the Avery situation, she'd decided that it would be easier to get the money through Robert. He told us they were planning to wed as soon as the estate was settled. Then, more sadly, he told us why he understood her insistence on a joint savings account. All the easier to take the money and run.

But a lot of it, I told Miss Avery, was guesswork, because Thelma/ Carol couldn't answer for herself.

"She hasn't been found yet?"

"No, ma'am," I said. "Abe called ahead, and the police threw up roadblocks to stop the truck, so she surprised them all by racing back to Zebulon and disappearing into the mine."

It had been something to see, the truck skidding to a halt at the main resort, just minutes ahead of the pursuing police cars.

Thelma had hit the ground running, straight to the old shed above the mine shafts. Three days and four search parties later, there was still no trace. They said she'd either gotten lost, hurt, or would surface when she got hungry enough.

Snow fell outside. For a few moments I stared at the flakes as they pushed against the window. And I smiled. After the hours of horror in the mine chamber, thinking I would never see another afternoon, all the little things I had taken for granted before were special. Falling snow, a hug from my mom, running down the street. All of it made me understand what Abe had said about riding the edge of life, something all of us do with every precious breath but never stop to think about until it's about to be taken away.

"Pretty, isn't it?"

Miss Avery had noticed my gaze and understood my smile.

"Yes, ma'am."

"Even for someone old like me," she said, "life is something you want to hold on to. I'm glad the doctors have decided I'm still a tough enough chicken that they're almost ready to predict my heart will outlast theirs."

We both fell silent again. I could guess what she was thinking.

Abe.

She sighed. "Abe and I had a long talk last night. Dr. James thinks that he'll live a while longer, too. How much, they're not willing to guess. But much of his health was worsening because of his worries about Robert and the ski resort. And now, of course, he can relax some."

I nodded.

"Poor man. Trying to protect his son by letting him continue the very crimes that threatened his life's work."

"Poor Robert, too," I said. "He told us it was killing him, but he couldn't find a way to stop."

"Abe was in much better spirits," Miss Avery said. "The tax people have nothing to charge Robert with because the inheritance hasn't come into effect yet. The military won't be pressing charges for unauthorized use of classified information. In fact, they're half happy that Robert proved the portable hologram machines could be so effective! And Abe is happy that Robert had made a decision to confess."

I started to say something in return, but I was interrupted by a series of loud bangs in the hallway.

My turn to sigh. "Joel again," I explained, "happy to have more caps. He thinks everyone in here likes it when he plays cowboys and Indians."

Miss Avery smiled. "We do. Sometimes it's too stuffy in here. People think we're so old that they have to tiptoe around us."

Joel wandered in, blowing smoke from his Colt revolver.

"That reminds me," Miss Avery began, "earlier you started to explain how Joel had helped you escape from the mine chamber. But we got sidetracked—"

"His guncaps," I grinned. "I had a big roll in my ski jacket, plus a rope I'd taken away from him. In the darkness, I found the wig and dress Thelma used when she dressed up as the ghost. Right beside the door, I scraped all the gunpowder into a pile beside the wig, hoping the hairs were fine enough to catch fire.

"Then I found a couple of stones to bang together. Finally a spark touched off the gunpowder, and sure enough, the wig started burning. Then I added the dress to the fire, and it grew big enough that my crutches would burn, and then I kept adding things until the door burned enough that I could kick a hole through. And Joel's rope—"

I winced as Joel fired a couple of rounds behind my head. But it would be a long time before I'd get mad at him for carrying that gun around.

"—and his rope came in handy a few times as I found my way out. There were extension cords that led to the chamber to give it power. All I had to do was follow them out."

Miss Avery clapped her hands in glee. "Great escape!"

She put her hands beneath her shawl.

Joel moved between us and brought his gun up to fire a final round at me.

"Hang on, pardner," Miss Avery drawled from behind him. "I got the drop on you."

Joel's face scrunched with confusion. He turned to face her, then dropped his gun.

Miss Avery had taken her own cap gun from beneath her shawl. She held it steady and snarled.

"That's right," she said. "Ever since your last visit, I've been prepared. Vamoose."

She fired a couple of shots at his feet that made him jump and run. I'd never seen Joel move so fast before.

Miss Avery winked at me. "What do you think we are, anyway—old geezers?"

Around the World With Christian Heroes!

TRAILBLAZER BOOKS give you an adventure story and an introduction to a Christian hero of the past. Whatever country or time interests you most, chances are there's a TRAILBLAZER BOOK about it. And each story is told through the eyes of a boy or girl your age. Be sure to travel the globe and go back through time with the TRAILBLAZER BOOKS.

TRAILBLAZER BOOKS by Dave and Neta Jackson

Abandoned on/Wild Frontier - Cartwright
Ambushed in Jaguar Swamp - Grubb
Assassins in the Cathedral - Kivengere
Attack in the Rye Grass - Whitman
The Bandit of Ashley Downs - Müller
The Betrayer's Fortune - Simons
Blinded by the Shining Path - Sauñe
Caught in the Rebel Camp - Douglass
The Chimney Sweep's Ransom - Wesley
Danger on the Flying Trapeze - Moody
Defeat of the Ghost Riders - Bethune
Drawn by a China Moon - Moon
The Drummer Boy's Battle - Nightingale
Escape From the Slave Traders - Livingstone
Exiled to the Red River - Garry
The Fate of the Yellow Woodbee - Saint
Flight of the Fugitives - Aylward
The Forty-Acre Swindle - Carver
The Gold Miner's Rescue - Jackson
The Hidden Jewel - Carmichael

Hostage on the Nighthawk - Penn
Imprisoned in the Golden City - Judson
Journey to the End of the Earth - Seymore
Kidnapped by River Rats - Booth
Listen for the Whippoorwill - Tubman
Mask of the Wolf Boy - Goforth
The Mayflower Secret - Bradford
The Queen's Smuggler - Tyndale
Quest for the Lost Prince - Morris
Race for the Record - Ridderhof
Risking the Forbidden Game - Cary
Roundup of the Street Rovers - Brace
The Runaway's Revenge - Newton
Shanghaied to China - Taylor
Sinking the Dayspring - Paton
Spy for the Night Riders - Luther
The Thieves of Tyburn Square - Fry
Traitor in the Tower -Bunyan
Trial by Poison - Slessor
The Warrior's Challenge - Zeisberger

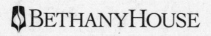

BETHANYHOUSE